MARTHA

By

Ruby Hopper

authorHOUSE

1663 Liberty Drive, Suite 200
Bloomington, Indiana 47403
(800) 839-8640
www.authorhouse.com

© 2004 Ruby Hopper
All Rights Reserved.

No part of this book may be reproduced, stored in a retrieval system, or transmitted by any means without the written permission of the author.

First published by AuthorHouse 08/03/04

ISBN: 1-4184-6143-1 (e)
ISBN: 1-4184-4525-8 (sc)
ISBN: 1-4184-4524-X (dj)

Library of Congress Control Number: 2003099867

Printed in the United States of America
Bloomington, Indiana

This book is printed on acid-free paper.

1 HAPPY NEW YEAR, 1848

Martha opened the door and watched the snow flakes swirling around John. He carried the gallon of fresh milk to the kitchen table. It wasn't daylight yet, but soon the children would be up, demanding breakfast. John went back to the barn, and finished his chores. He returned with enough milk for his family, and today's guests.

"Oh, it's cold," John said. "This is as bad as the winters in Boston. Now, what are we having for breakfast? I'm starving. Can you fix some of Malindy's gravy? You know, the one with the funny name."

"Oh, you mean 'Poor Do Gravy?'" Martha said. "You're always hungry, John," she teased. "But it sure would taste good with my biscuits, wouldn't it?"

John was chilled to the bone. He poured himself some coffee, and sat down by the fireplace. He smiled, as he thought of all the coffee they'd had to drink on the 1843 wagon train. His thoughts were interrupted by the sound of little feet running across the floor.

"Mommie, Mommie," Johnny cried, as he ran past his father. Martha picked him up, kissing his tasseled forehead.

"Johnny, are you ready for company today?" she asked, as he squealed with delight.

While Martha fed him, John attended to the baby. In a few minutes, he brought Carolyn into the kitchen, and exchanged duties with Martha.

I remember when I thought children were so uncouth Martha reminded herself. *I can't believe I almost let those preconceived notions ruin my life. Thank You God, for my two wonderful children.* She hummed a spontaneous melody as she rocked her baby.

"What time will our guests arrive?" John asked.

"Malindy said they'd be here around noon," Martha said."But Sarah and Bobby have the longest drive."

Martha began preparing her share of the New Years Day meal. She'd always enjoyed hosting dinner parties, and this task made her happy.

"Just look at it snow," John said. "Should I go check on any of our guests? In weather like this, they could lose their way."

"Wait a little while before you do that," Martha said. She took the lid off the big Dutch skillet, and the aroma of roast venison filled the cabin. Her taste test confirmed the doneness and flavor of the meat. She sat it on the table.

"This reminds me so much of Grandma Catherine," she said. "I sure do miss her. There's so much I want to tell her."

They welcomed Calvin and Malindy Miller, with their children. Many times Calvin and Malindy had come to their rescue, helping and encouraging them with almost parental devotion. Calvin and John shook hands, while Malindy hugged Martha. The Miller children began playing with Johnny and Carolyn. John took the big kettle of food from Calvin, and sat it on the kitchen table.

"Well, how've you been?" Malindy said.

"We're doing just fine," Martha said. "Haven't seen you since Christmas, and I've missed you. John's law firm is well established. The new lawyer that just moved here is no competition at all, now. The kids are both all right, and we're happy. So, how've you all been?"

"We're just fine, too," Malindy said. "Willie's got him a hack job, now. Course, I reckon you and John see him and that buggy of his all over the place. He's keeping company with that Betty Sue Butler. And I got me a hunch they just may tie the knot, if she thinks she can put up with him. Johnny and Oliver's hauling logs over to Frank Parkers' saw mill. They live off up there close to the mill. Sarah and Bobby's got another one on the way, and my least one's still at home. Becky and Jenny moved into the Boarding House. Tommy keeps me and Calvin company. It'd sure be mighty lonesome around the house without him."

"Come on in, Carolyn," John said, as he shook hands with James Greene. James took their food basket to the table. Carolyn went straight for her namesake, Carolyn Campbell.

"My, how you've grown," Carolyn said, holding Martha's daughter.

I want my baby to love her as much as I always have Martha thought. She knew her parents still resented that their servants, James and Carolyn left Boston for the wilds of the new Oregon Territory. *Oh well, if they don't like it, there's nothing they can do about it now* she mused.

Soon more guests arrived. John greeted Big Jim and Helen Cross, Susan and Patrick McDonald, Sarah and Bobby Parker. They all brought more children and food. Becky came with Billy Joe McCavendish, and Jenny was escorted by Charles Price.

This was a happy occasion, a New Years celebration with family and friends. The men gathered by the fireplace, talking politics, weather, and farming. The women congregated around the kitchen table, where Malindy had taken charge of the cooking. The house was full of family, children, good friends, and laughter. Martha thought this is really how life should be.

"What's this?" Susan asked, pointing to Malindy's entree.

"Why, that there's hog jaw and black-eyed peas," she said. "It brings you good luck all year, if you eat this on New Years Day. It's mighty good with cornbread, fried 'taters, and a great big onion."

"Oh, I'm afraid Patrick would never permit me to serve another potato," Susan said.

Malindy gave her a sample. Then she just had to have the recipe.

"Dinner," Martha announced. Immediately the kitchen was over run with a mob of hungry people, each wanting to be first in line. Martha regained control, and established a pecking order.

"All right, older kids, help the smaller ones, then you can eat," Martha said. "Calvin, would you ask the Blessing?"

Every head bowed, and hats were removed as Calvin spoke. "Lord, we thank You for all this food, for our families and friends, and for keeping us all together, and safe. Amen."

They attacked the mountain of food as if they'd gone hungry for a week. Martha felt a wonderful happiness and satisfaction at seeing everyone enjoying themselves. How different from the social circles she'd grown up with in Boston. Martha caught John's eye. He gave her a wink, and a big smile of approval.

"How's things at the Sheriff's Office?" John asked Big Jim.

"Kind of slow," Jim said, through a mouthful of Martha's roast. "It's sure a lot different than being a wagon scout. I think this snow's kept everybody in, and that suits me just fine."

"Well, Carolyn, what's going on at your Boarding House?" Malindy said.

Martha noted that Malindy's backwoods English was still intact. She felt comforted by all those colloquial expressions. What did it matter if Malindy ruptured the King's English? Malindy had a heart full of love, bigger than the whole Oregon Territory, and that's what really mattered to Martha. She listened as Carolyn spoke of her business venture.

"Oh, we're doing so well," she said. She was proud of their accomplishments. For the first time in their lives, James and Carolyn had something they could call their own. "James fixed up another room, and we rented it last week."

Carolyn turned to Susan, and continued. "Susan, I've been thinking. I need someone to help me cook. Would you and Helen like to help me? I can't pay you much right now. But I know things will improve."

"Yes, I'd love to," Susan said. "When can we start?"

"I'd love to help you, too," Helen said. "But what about our children?"

"Oh, just bring them along with you," Carolyn said. "You know I love them to pieces. It's all settled, then. You can both start tomorrow. Just be there around five in the morning."

"Has anybody seen Aunt Susie? Or Henry and Minnie?" Malindy asked.

"They came by to see us just before Christmas," Helen said. "They'd just went and got his Mother, and brought her out here. She sure is a sweet little lady."

"Just when will I see their little girl in school?" Martha said.

"Well, she's only a year old, you know," Helen said.

"Did you know Sally Connelly has a laundry house in Oregon City?" Carolyn said.

Everyone was surprised at this news.

"I seen Jerry back in the fall," Bobby said. "He was working with Sam Barlow, cutting that road over Mt. Hood."

John asked if Jerry gave out much information about himself or Sally.

"No, not really," Bobby said. "He was friendly enough, and asked about all of us, especially Minnie and Henry. Him and Sally's got two little boys, now. He said they go see Aunt Susie every once in a while."

6

"We got some really bad news from Ireland," Susan said. "Patrick's uncle said there's a terrible famine, and several of our folks are sick. I didn't mean to say anything about this, but I'm so afraid. Patrick is just beside himself with worry."

"Oh, no, honey," Carolyn said. "How bad is it?"

"Very bad," she said. "We haven't heard from home in three years. I wrote my mother last week, but I'm almost afraid to get an answer."

"Martha, are you going to teach again this year?" Calvin said.

"Yes," Martha said. "I think we can get in three months of school, March, April and May."

"What's it like at Oregon Institute?" Jenny Miller asked. She didn't know how this question would be received by her parents, or Charles. But Jenny had a great thirst for knowledge.

"Well, it's only been established for two or three years, now," Martha said. "I haven't been over there, and I don't think I know anyone there. Jenny, are you interested in attending the Oregon Institute?"

"Yeah, I think so," Jenny said. "What all do I have to do?"

Before a surprised Martha could answer, Jenny's sister, Becky echoed the same desire. Malindy and Calvin were momentarily speechless. This also caught the two young men off guard. The girls had said nothing about this to anyone.

"Girls, I'll be glad to help you," Martha said. "We'll get started immediately. I still have my old books, and we can use them." Martha was very pleased with the Miller girls.

Calvin finally found his voice.

"Girls, why didn't you tell us?" he said. "I don't know what your Ma thinks, but I'm all for it."

"Martha, do they even let girls go to this school?" Malindy asked.

"Yes, they do," she said. "I've heard there are several women students."

"Now girls," Malindy said. "Me and your Pa never had a chance to go to school much. But you do. I agree with your Pa, I'm all for it. I want you to do the best you can, and learn all you can. I'm so proud of you both I could just bust."

"What do you think, Billy Joe?" Calvin said.

"I don't know," he said. "I guess it'd be all right. I never did go to school much. But I guess maybe one of us ought to be smart."

"How about you, Charles? What do you think?" Calvin said.

"How you going to pay for all this?" he said. "I ain't got no money, and I don't think you do, either."

"Just leave that to me," Martha said.

Growing up in a privileged society, Martha's education was always the finest available. Her father spared no expense, sending her to study in Paris, London, and New York. But this was still a frontier settlement, not yet even part of the United States. This family had no money, and enrollment just might be difficult. But Martha resolved to stand by these girls.

"Now, how about some of my gooseberry pie?" Malindy said.

"What is a 'gooseberry'?" Martha said.

As the pie was passed around, Malindy explained the tart little green berry.

After the meal, the ladies washed and put away the dishes. There was no food left over, and nothing was wasted. The men helped John carry in more wood, and feed his livestock.

"John, do you think Oregon will ever become a state?" Patrick said.

"Yes. Someday it will," he said. "Mr. Meeker and Dr. McLoughlin have already done most of the preliminary work. I know President Polk wants to get England out of the Oregon Territory this year, as well as from those little islands off the coast. Back in '46, President Polk gave them a one year notice of termination of joint occupancy. I read in the newspaper from Boston that England almost went to war with us over this."

"You don't think they'll fight us, do you?" Big Jim said.

"No. But they sure don't want to give this up," John said.

"I sure don't want to sell my cows to the British," Bobby said. "Say, Jim, I may need your help with a cattle drive this fall."

"Sure, Bobby," Jim said. "I'd be glad to help you. What are you planning to do?"

"Well, I thought I'd go back to where the old cattle trail meets the Oregon Road at the Ogalalla Village. I figure to get me a big herd, and bring them back here. What I want to know is, why can't we cut right straight across the Territory from Fort Boise? That way, I wouldn't have to take them on the Columbia River. What do you think, Jim?"

"Yeah, I think that'll work, Bobby," he said. "But there ain't no trail that I know of. You'll just have to cut your own trail."

9

"I think I can do that," Bobby said.

John continued his conversation with the others regarding Oregon statehood. They all agreed with him.

"The 1818 Convention established the Oregon boundary lines," he said. "And I know the President isn't happy with it. This may take him a year or two, but I believe he can do it."

All afternoon, the children played in the snow, throwing snowballs, and making a snow man. Martha opened the door for a moment, and watched Johnny as he played and laughed with the others. Their laughter filled the air, and there was joy in Martha's heart.

They talked until late afternoon. Then one by one, they said good bye. The snow had stopped, and each family wanted to get home before dark. John and Martha escorted James and Carolyn out to their wagon. Carolyn hugged Martha and the children, then John helped her into the wagon.

John checked on the livestock, then came back to the cabin. He stopped, and brushed the snow off the gate, revealing the *Possum Hollow* name plaque. His father had ridiculed the name, and Martha's father didn't like it, either. But this was not their parents home. It belonged to John and Martha Campbell, and they liked *Possum Hollow*.

John came inside the cabin, and saw Martha setting by the fire, knitting.

"I've really enjoyed this day," he said. "We had a good time in Possum Hollow today, didn't we?"

"Yes, we did," Martha said. "Let's get to bed earlier tonight. Remember, you have an eight o'clock appointment in the morning."

2 THE QUEEN OF HEARTS

She sat in John's office with an angry, defiant look. Big Jim had placed her in handcuffs. She was still resistant, kicking at anyone who came near her.

John read Jim's notes on her arrest. He couldn't help but wonder why such an attractive woman would resort to killing her husband. According to the notes, she'd been married to three other men. Each of them died under unusual circumstances.

"Mrs. Edwards," John said. "Do you understand that you're being charged with the murder of your husband, Phillip Edwards?"

"Murder?" she yelled. "I didn't kill him. He died of that there disease he had as a boy."

"Well, ma'am, his brother up at Mt. Hood said he'd never been sick a day in his life," John pointed out. "How do you explain this contradiction?"

"Why, Phillip told me about it before we was ever married," she said. "It was some kind of fever that left him with a bad heart. He never could do much work, cause he'd get out of breath real bad. He just keeled over, dead as a door nail."

John sensed that she was lying. "Now, Mrs. Edwards," John said sternly, "if you want me to defend you, you have to be honest with me. If I find that you're not being honest, I'll withdraw from this case immediately. Do you understand?"

"Yeah," she muttered. "I understand."

"All right, let's start at the beginning," John said, taking out his notebook. "Tell me everything you can remember about the night of December twentieth."

"Well," she sniffed, "we'd just finished supper. I was cleaning up my pots and pans, and he went out to the barn to feed the stock. After a while, when he didn't come back, I went out to look for him. I found him in the barn, dead. And that's all I know, honest."

"Is there anyone who can back you up?" John said.

"Are you calling me a liar?" she screamed, kicking his desk.

"No. I'm not calling you a liar, Mrs. Edwards," John said calmly. He was beginning to wish he'd never agreed to defend her. "You'll need someone who can verify that you're telling the truth. Can you think of anyone who might be able to help you?"

"Well, my cousin, RubyAnn Caster lives up at that new settlement at the mouth of the Willamette River. Portland, they call it. Me and her growed up together, and I reckon she knows me about as well as anybody."

"I'd like to talk to her," John said. "If you think of anyone else, please let me know." He asked a few more questions, then went over his notes with her.

"Mrs. Edwards, I need you to sign this statement," John said. "All this does is verify the things you've told me are correct and true, and that you're being honest. Please read it before you sign it."

She glanced through the notes, hardly reading anything. Then Pauline Edwards scrawled her name and the date on the last page. John countersigned, and Big Jim added his signature as Sheriff.

Big Jim walked toward her, and Pauline knew he'd be taking her back to jail.

"Whoa, here," Pauline said. "I ain't going back to that jail. There's bugs and mice in there. And it's ice cold, to boot."

"Mrs. Edwards, you don't have much choice," John said. "Right now, the Oregon Territory doesn't have much of a legal system, and there's no other place for you to stay. Sometimes we can get a judge to come from back east, but that takes a long time. I'm sorry, but this is the best we can do."

Big Jim offered to help her to her feet, but she shoved him away. "I don't need your help," she snarled.

Turning back to John, she said, "Mr. Campbell, you got to make them let me go. Get me out of that stinking jail."

After they left, John went over his notes again. He didn't like Pauline Edwards, and he certainly didn't trust her. He knew she was lying. He needed more information, the sooner, the better. *I know I'm suppose to give her the benefit of the doubt* he thought. *What if she did kill him? I don't ever want to be in that kind of situation again.* John paced the floor another half an hour, pondering all the possible explanations for this death. Finally, he remembered two more people who might have some information.

He would start with Willie's Dearborn carriage. Willie's taxi hauled many people every day, and he could always hear his passengers' conversations. John knew the passengers would sometimes confide things to Willie, trusting him with all kinds of secrets. New settlers always stayed at Carolyn's Boarding House until they could build their own cabins. Perhaps some of the guests might have heard something.

John put on his best bib and tucker, got his hat and coat, and walked up the street. James rode by. He was hauling logs for another addition to the boarding house. He stopped and talked to John.

"Back in November, there were two families that stayed with us," James said. "They talked about traveling with the Edwards's. I didn't get to hear much, but I don't think they liked her. They seemed to think Phillip was a good man, though."

"Did they say anything about her three other marriages?" John asked.

"No. Just that they felt sorry for Phillip."

"Do you have the names of these people?"

"Sure. Ride with me to the house, and I'll show you the register," James said.

John visited briefly with James and Carolyn, then James brought the guest register. John copied names, and went into town to locate them. He collected evidence all afternoon. His notebook was filling up with facts against Pauline. Still, he kept hoping someone would take Pauline's side. No one did.

"Howdy, John," Willie said. "Need a ride?"

"I sure do, Willie," he said. "Drive me back to the office, and we'll talk."

John climbed inside, and greeted the other passengers. As Willie continued his route, John marveled at Willie's knack for always landing on his feet.

Two years ago, Willie started his taxi wagon in Oregon City with one old beat up farm wagon and two mules. He'd rebuilt the wagon with scrap parts scavenged from other broken down wagons. He braced the old wagon bed, and put a good canvas on top. Inside, he'd partitioned it into a very comfortable seating area. Now he'd added two Dearborns, mud wagons, more mules, and two new drivers. John smiled as he thought of Willie's ability to make a dollar. He remembered Willie's antics on the 1843 wagon train that brought them all here. *Who would have thought it then? Mr. Willie Miller is going to be just fine, thank you very much* John thought.

Willie escorted the last passengers to their cabin. He helped Mr. Johnson carry two fifty-pound sacks of flour. Then he returned to his carriage.

As they entered the office, John got right to the point.

"Willie, have you heard anything about Phillip and Pauline Edwards?" John wasn't looking for gossip and rumors, and never depended on that. But there's an element of truth in even the wildest rumor. It was his job to separate the wheat from the chaff.

Willie told him everything he could remember. It was beginning to look very bad for Pauline. He also mentioned Pauline's cousin, RubyAnn.

"You might want to talk to her, John," he said. "I think she knows a lot more than she's letting on."

"Would you be willing to drive me up there? I hear they've got a better macadam road now," John said.

They scheduled the trip for Friday morning. Willie returned to his work, and John went home to Possum Hollow.

Friday morning, Willie's carriage pulled into Possum Hollow. John helped Martha get the children seated, then he sat down beside her. The trip would take all day, and they'd have to find a place to spend the night. John was hoping Willie could suggest some place comfortable. He was anxious to get there, and find RubyAnn. Martha was anxious to go shopping with the children.

The new road had just recently been carved out of the wilderness, and it was rough. Martha compared it to Rock Avenue along the Oregon Trail. Memories of that trip filled her mind, as she looked out the crude window. The carriage rolled over a deep rut, waking up the baby, and she began to cry. Martha calmed her down by singing to her, as she rocked back and forth.

"You all right back there?" Willie said.

"Yes, we're fine," John said.

When they arrived at the settlement, they stopped at the Sheriff's office. John went inside to inquire about RubyAnn. Martha and the children went across the street to the General Merchandise.

"Are you RubyAnn Caster?" John asked the little bar maid.

"Yeah. What's it to you, honey?" came her raspy answer. She turned to face him.

John was abashed. *Why, she can't be more than twenty years old* John thought. *She'd be much more attractive with less make-up.* Still, she was pretty, with lovely dark brown hair.

"My name is John Campbell. I'm an attorney for Pauline Edwards," John said.

"Ha! What's she done now?"

"Her husband, Phillip has been murdered."

"She done it," RubyAnn said empathically. "Betcha my last dollar, she done it."

"Well, I'd like to think she's innocent, until proven otherwise," John said. He wanted to see how much information RubyAnn would volunteer.

"Innocent, my foot," RubyAnn said, getting a little agitated. "She just marries these men for their money, then gets rid of them when the money runs out."

"How do you know that for certain?" John asked.

"Listen, honey," she continued, as she served a drink to her customer. "I know what kind of person she really is. After all, I growed up with her back in Richmond. When we was just kids, she was mean as the devil then. And she's still meaner than a junk yard dog."

"Oh, really?" John said.

"Now, I ain't no saint. And I never did claim to be, either," she said. "I'm right ashamed of myself at how I really make a living."

RubyAnn pointed to a corner table. "Let's set over there, honey. We can talk more without everybody hearing us."

They sat down, and she offered him a shot of whiskey. John declined, requesting coffee instead. RubyAnn drank the whiskey she'd offered him, then poured herself another shot.

"Smart man," she said, complementing his refusal of the whiskey. "Your Mommie must've raised you right. Take it from me, honey, never get started on this stuff."

She got up and brought him a cup of coffee, and their conversation continued.

"How well did you know Phillip?"

"He was a good man," she said. "I liked him, cause he always treated me like a lady. He never did call me a tramp, like some of the other men did. He never said an unkind word to nobody. And, I guess he must have really loved Pauline, cause he never did do nothing bad. If he had done something bad, I would've heard about it."

"How did she treat him?"

"Like a dog," she said in disgust. RubyAnn took out a little tobacco pouch that she kept tucked inside her petticoat. She arranged the tobacco on thin paper, then rolled it into a cigarette. She looked around for a match, but finding none, she opened the door of the old pot bellied stove. With the poker, she carefully raked some coals up close to the door. She touched the cigarette to the coals. A second later, she brought it to her lips, and drew a long puff. She blew the smoke away from John.

"I like you, honey," she said, patting his hand. "And I don't want you to smell like this old cigarette."

John was getting embarrassed.

RubyAnn continued. "Poor old Phillip. He didn't even last till he was all gone," she said, shaking her head. "Still, he lasted longer than the other men she had."

"Pauline said he had a heart attack," John said. "Was he ever in bad health?"

"Not that I ever knowed of," she said. "I bet she poisoned him, or something like that."

"Do you think she killed him?" John asked. He thought he knew what her reply would be, but he needed to hear her say it for the record.

"Yeah. I think she killed him, just like she done away with all the others," RubyAnn said. "Like I said, honey, I ain't no saint. But at least, I ain't never killed nobody."

John didn't want to leave any room for doubt. "Are you sure she killed the other men, too?"

"Heck, yeah. I'm sure she did it," she said, waving hello to another man at the bar. "Back in Richmond, she'd get real drunk, and brag about it to me and my sister. Everybody around Richmond knowed about it. And the law couldn't do nothing about it, cause they couldn't prove it. Nobody would ever tell what they knowed, cause she would've killed them, too. Some of the men tried to keep old Phillip from marrying her. Bet he wishes now he'd listened to them."

RubyAnn got up and walked to the bar, then poured a drink for the man she'd waved at. She shouted to the bar tender to bring in more Jack Daniels. She returned to John, and continued her story.

"Tiny always uses moonshine," she said, laughing. "He keeps them old Jack Daniels bottles, pours the 'shine in them, and sells it as the pure Jack. He'd fire me for sure, if he knowed I told you that. But seeing as how you don't drink it anyway, I don't see no harm in telling you."

"Why did Phillip and Pauline come to Oregon City?" John said.

"Why, she got so mean nobody could stand her," RubyAnn said, sipping the whiskey. "She threatened to kill anybody that told on her. And when she was drunk, she was a mean little wild cat, let me tell you. She got so bad the constable finally had to run her and Phillip out of town. And that's when they come here."

This was more than enough information to convict Pauline. John knew he could never defend her. The best Pauline could hope for was mercy from the judge, plead guilty, and ask for leniency.

John paid RubyAnn for her time. He gently shook her hand, put his hat on, and stood up to leave.

"Thank you, RubyAnn," he said. "You've really been a big help."

As he walked to the door, she called to him.

"Mr. Campbell, wait…" She took his hand, and returned the ten dollar gold coin.

"Your wife is the luckiest woman on earth," she said. "If I had me a good man like you, I'd be walking in high cotton, for sure."

"But I didn't tell you a thing about myself," John said. "How do you know I'm married?"

"You didn't have to say anything," she said, smiling at him. "I can tell by the way you talk and act. If I ever need me a good lawyer, I'll sure call you." Standing on tiptoes, she kissed his cheek.

The bar room erupted in cat calls, wolf whistles, and laughter as John walked out the door. He was embarrassed. But he couldn't hold back the giggles when he heard RubyAnn yell, "Oh, shut up." More laughter and cheers accompanied her remark.

Martha wasn't having any shopping success. She could find more things in Oregon City than here. But it was always fun exploring a new town, and meeting new people. She purchased some yarn, intending to make herself a new shawl. Why not make one for her Mother? That would make a nice gift to take her someday.

John caught up with Martha as they came out of the General Merchandise store. They found Willie, and began looking for a good place to eat.

"There's a good Boarding House and café just up the street here," Willie said. "When I come up here, I always go there."

They finished their meal, and made arrangements to spend the night. As they prepared the children for bed, John related his conversation with RubyAnn.

"Deep inside, she's honest and good," he said. "If she'd had someone to lean on, and help her, she would have been a fine woman. When I left, she gave the money back to me. She said if she had a man like me, she'd be 'walking in high cotton', whatever that is."

The next morning, they left early. Willie was anxious to get back home. Martha surmised that he was missing Betty Sue. Martha was sure missing Possum Hollow.

Finally Willie announced, "Possum Hollow, coming up."

John paid Willie, and helped Martha and the children get out of the carriage. Willie drove away, while John got his family inside.

John got to the Sheriff's office before Big Jim arrived. He stood on the porch, waiting. At last, he saw Jim riding into town.

"Howdy, John," Big Jim said, as he tied his horse to the hitching post. "Anything wrong?"

"Well, no, not exactly," John said. "But I do need to tell you what I found out about Pauline. Can we talk privately?"

"Sure, John," he said. "Let's walk over to the lumber yard. There ain't no body there at this time of the morning. What'd you find out?"

John recounted RubyAnn's information, and the other things he'd learned.

"I believe RubyAnn, Jim. There's no possible way I could honestly defend Pauline. I'm going to advise her to plead guilty, ask for mercy, and just take her punishment. What do you think, Jim?"

"Well, I thought she killed him, too," Big Jim said. "Doc Brown couldn't find any marks on him anywhere. No bullet wounds, no stab wounds. He said it didn't look like a heart attack to him. But what are we going to do with her, John? She's yelling and screaming all the time. And it's driving me crazy."

"Maybe I should go talk to Mr. Meeker. I hope we can work something out with the Provisional Government Office," John said..

"I sure hope so," Jim said. "You aim to tell her today?"

"No. I'll wait till I see Mr. Meeker," John said. "But I want you to be there when I do tell her. I'd also like to have a third person there–someone who doesn't know any of us. I want a reliable account of what I tell her."

"Well, how about Mr. Rowland?" Jim said. "I heard they just moved in here from New York. I don't know the man myself, but I've heard he's a mighty fine fellow."

"That's good," John said. "I don't know him, either. And I'm sure Pauline doesn't. I'll ride up to see Mr. Meeker in the morning. See if you can find Mr. Rowland, and we'll all meet here at noon."

John explained his case to Mr. Meeker.

"Well, John," Mr. Meeker said. "About the only thing I can do is to suggest that Pauline be taken up to Fort Vancouver. They have a better jail there. I'll send one of my men down to Oregon City to get her. Have a full report written up, and we'll send that with her. Sometimes they take a bunch of prisoners back east, and maybe they'll take her."

John thanked him. He felt relieved, and thought this would be best for all of them. But he was afraid Pauline might not take this news very well.

John chatted with Mr. Rowland, exchanging pleasantries. Big Jim brought Pauline out of the cell, and into his office. He introduced her to Mr. Rowland, then clicked the handcuffs on her wrists.

"Hey, watch it there," Pauline said. "Them things hurt. Mr. Campbell, make him take them things off of me."

23

"Pauline, please set down," John said firmly.

"Now, you're my lawyer. Make him get them things off of me," she demanded again.

"Set down, Pauline. If you don't, the Sheriff will put you back in that cell," John said.

She sat down. Pauline was angry, and she felt trapped. She took her anger out on Mr. Rowland.

"What are you doing here?" Pauline asked.

"He's here as a witness to what I'm going to tell you," John said. He confronted Pauline with all the evidence against her.

"Pauline, you lied to me," John said. "Remember what I told you about that?"

"I thought you was supposed to help me get out of jail," Pauline said. "Ain't that what a lawyer's for?"

"That's only part of my job," John said. "My job requires that I find out the truth. I really believe you killed Phillip. I don't know exactly how you did it, but whatever you did caused his death. As your attorney, it's my duty to give you the best legal advice I can. I believe you should plead guilty, ask for the courts leniency, and accept the sentence of the Provisional Government."

"What?" Pauline shouted. "I will not. Some lawyer you are. I could've done better than this myself."

"Mrs. Edwards, perhaps it would be best…" Mr. Rowland said.

"You stay out of my business," Pauline said. She kicked his legs so hard that he was doubled up in pain. Mr. Rowland started to hit her.

"That's enough," Big Jim said. He grabbed Rowland's arm, and pulled him away from her.

"Pauline, you don't have much choice," John said.

She spit in his face. John took out a handkerchief, and cleaned his cheek.

"You can't hide from yourself, Pauline," John said. "You have to face this, even if it does mean time in jail."

"There are good jails back in…." Mr. Rowland tried to tell her.

"I ain't going," she said emphatically. "You might as well let me go, cause you ain't taking me to no jail."

"Yes, we will," Big Jim said. He helped her up, and pushed her back to the cell.

John thanked Mr. Rowland, and he left.

"Jim, I'll have the papers ready for you in the morning," John said. They could hear Pauline yelling at them.

"I'll sure be glad to get rid of her," Big Jim said.

3 CAROLYN'S BOARDING HOUSE

"**S**omebody make that kid shut up," Mr. Johnson said. "It's three o'clock in the morning, and I'd like to go back to bed."

James got up, and walked to the door. He couldn't imagine what all the fuss was about. There was no one with children staying at Carolyn's Boarding House. He heard a door slam, and thought it was Mr. Johnson. Half asleep, James went back to bed.

"I had the strangest dream last night," James said, as they dressed. "I dreamed we have a baby in the house."

"You haven't had any of Malindy's potions, have you," Carolyn teased.

James laughed, then went to the wood shed. He brought back enough wood for the day. Then he went to the hen house for eggs. As he returned with the fragile cargo, he heard the baby crying again.

I must be losing what little sense I've got James thought. *I know we don't have anyone here with a baby.*

As James came to the back porch, he saw Carolyn picking up a basket.

"What's in the basket?" James said.

"James, look at this poor little baby. She's so cold she's turning blue," Carolyn said. "Open the door, and we'll get her inside."

"Where did this child come from?" James said. Now he knew what Mr. Johnson heard last night.

"I don't know," Carolyn said. "I heard her crying, and came out here. Do you suppose her Mother needs a place to stay?"

They carried her to the kitchen table, and Carolyn picked her up. She inspected the child for any signs of injury or frostbite. The child appeared normal and healthy.

James looked in the basket. It was well lined with blankets, but no milk, food, or toys. Then he saw the note.

"Here's a note," he said, unfolding the paper. "It says, 'I know you're good people, and will take care of her. My wife died in childbirth. I can't raise her by myself. We named her Jane.'"

Carolyn dipped her finger in a cup of milk, and kept a steady drip from her finger into the baby's mouth. They forgot everything else, as they fed their new guest.

James heard Susan enter the kitchen, and realized they needed to prepare breakfast for the other guests.

"Susan's already here, and Helen will be here in a few minutes," James said.

"Good," Carolyn said. "Maybe they can help take care of her."

All the other guests, except Mr. Johnson, took turns feeding and rocking her until breakfast was served. They all read the note, and tried to think of who the parents might be.

"Strange that none of us heard about a woman dying in childbirth," Susan said.

"Maybe we should ask Willie if he's heard anything," Helen said.

That evening, Willie stopped to visit James and Carolyn.

"I ain't got no idea who could've left her," he said. "She's a mighty pretty little thing, ain't she? How in the world could anybody just leave her alone like that?" He promised to tell Bobby to bring extra milk, then left for home.

John drove his buggy home, and unhitched the horse. He gathered an armload of firewood, and went inside.

"Somebody left a baby at the Boarding House," he told Martha. He helped her carry the big Dutch oven to the table, and related all he'd heard about the baby. They discussed the baby's plight for several minutes, then John changed the subject.

"There's another wagon train coming this year," John said. "I heard Franklin Patton is going to be the wagon scout. I can't wait to see him."

"I'm sure he'll have news from Boston," Martha said.

Resting at the table for a moment, John thought about Boston, and all the finer things of life.

"Everybody thought we were crazy to come here," he said. "Especially Father and Charles. But this is the way people ought to live, Martha. It's so peaceful and quiet. We have everything we want and need. That's what really makes a person successful."

After the evening meal, they played with the children until bedtime.

"Martha, I've been thinking," John said. "How would you like to have a new house?"

"Oh, I'd love it," she said.

"I want more room for our children," John said. "Besides, I did promise you the best home in Oregon."

"I love this cabin, John," she said. "I love it because you built it for us. It's our *home*."

There's something about the word *home* that conveys a deep, almost spiritual meaning. Home can be a tent under a tree, a cave, a house, a castle. Martha realized the quality that makes a building a home is love. Martha had a home filled with love, and it always gave her great comfort. Martha fell asleep, still thinking of things that make a home.

As John walked to his office, he knew someone was swiftly catching up with him. *Oh, no. The good councilman is early today* John thought, referring to Councilman Dudley. Mr. Dudley frequently made a pest of himself at every business in town. He would show up without notice, interrupting business transactions, or scheduled appointments. He would talk aimlessly for an hour or more. Many times this had made John late. Sometimes he tried to excuse himself, and just walk away. But Mr. Dudley would follow him, talking constantly. Malindy said Mr. Dudley was like some 'old gossipie woman' she knew. John agreed with that description.

"Good morning, Mr. Dudley," John said.

"Shame about that baby, John," he said. "What's the matter with young people today? When I was a boy, folks took care of their own. Any idea who done this, John?"

"No, not yet," John said. "Mr. Dudley, I've got…"

"Here, John," Mr. Dudley said. "The wife sent you some of her prize winning apple pie. Now, the secret's in the spices she uses. And that crust is something, too. Here, John, take a bite of this," he said, handing the pie to John.

"Yes, Mr. Dudley. She makes delicious pies," John agreed. Truth was, her pie was exceptionally good, but John had an appointment coming any moment. He had no idea how to politely get Mr. Dudley to leave. He looked at the clock on the wall. It was time for Mr. Peterson, the Provisional Government deputy who would take Pauline Edwards to Fort Vancouver.

John found the papers he needed to give Mr. Peterson. Mr. Dudley sat down on the corner of the desk. He gave John another piece of pie.

"Best pie in the world, ain't it, John?" Mr. Dudley said, as he shoved the pie in John's mouth.

"Yes, indeed," John said.

Mr. Peterson came into the office.

"I'm looking for either Sheriff Cross, or John Campbell," he said. "My name is William Peterson, and I'm here to escort your prisoner to Fort Vancouver." He extended his hand to greet John.

John still had that pie in his mouth, and frantically began chewing it. He swallowed hard, then shook hands with Peterson.

"I'm John Campbell, Pauline's attorney," he said. "Please excuse me, I just had some of Mrs. Dudley's apple pie..."

"Would you like a piece?" Mr. Dudley said. "Best apple pie in the world. Isn't it, John?"

John was getting very annoyed with Councilman Dudley.

"Mr. Peterson, I'll take you over to the Sheriff's office. I believe Big Jim has everything ready, so please follow me." He handed his paperwork to Mr. Peterson, and they left. Mr. Dudley was right behind them.

"Mr. Peterson, this prize winning apple pie really is the best in the world," Mr. Dudley said. He pushed a slice of pie into Peterson's mouth.

"See? What'd I tell you? Good, isn't it? Huh, Peterson?" Mr. Dudley said.

"Yes, it's very good, sir," Mr. Peterson said. "Campbell, what on God's green earth is this man doing here?"

"Mr. Dudley, please," John said. "We have to transport a prisoner. It might be dangerous, and you really shouldn't be here."

They arrived at Big Jim's office with Mr. Dudley explaining the art and craft of his wife's baking talents.

"Morning, Sheriff," Mr. Dudley said. "Would you like to try a piece of Samantha's best apple pie. It's won Blue Ribbon Awards at every county fair. Here, try this." He thrust a slice of pie into Big Jim's face.

"Jim, this is Mr. Peterson," John said. "He's here to escort Pauline to Fort Vancouver."

Big Jim didn't like Mrs. Dudley's pies. Her secret spices always made him sick. He usually just held the pie in his mouth until he could turn around

31

and spit it out. But now he had to talk, so he swallowed it. He knew in a few minutes he'd be sick.

"Nice to meet you, Peterson," Jim said. "I'm Jim Cross, the Sheriff in Oregon City. I'll bring Pauline out, and you can get started."

"Thank you, Sheriff," he said. "But I'd really appreciate it if you would go with me to Fort Vancouver. Sometimes these prisoners get pretty hard for one man to handle, and I would really like some help. I'm authorized by Mr. Meeker and Dr. McLoughlin to pay you for it."

"Well, I guess that'd be ok," Jim said. "Nothing going on here today, anyway."

Big Jim brought Pauline out.

"Pauline, this is Mr. Peterson, from the Provisional Government Office," John said.

"What do you want?" Pauline said.

"The Sheriff and I are taking you up to Fort Vancouver," Peterson said.

"Hey, is that apple pie?" Pauline said. "Boy, that smells good. Can I have a slice of that?"

"Why, sure," Mr. Dudley said. "Best pie in the world, ain't it, John?" He gave her the last big slice.

"Let's get going," Big Jim said. He needed fresh air. Those secret spices were churning his stomach, and his head began to hurt.

"You got anymore pie?" Pauline said. "Best meal I've ever had in this stinking place."

"Come on, Pauline," Jim said. "We've got to go." He pushed her forward, and made her walk ahead of him.

"I can get you another pie," Mr. Dudley said. "It'll only take a minute. My house is just around the corner from the wash house."

"I don't think they have time to eat anymore," John said.

"If you ain't got a pie, how about some ham and biscuits?" Pauline said. "Anything would beat what I've had to put up with in there."

Big Jim excused himself, went behind the building and got sick.

"What's the matter with him?" Pauline said.

"Shut up, lady." Mr. Peterson said.

Big Jim returned, and stood in front of Mr. Dudley. "If you ever bring any more of her pies, or any of her cooking around me again, so help me, I'll shoot you both. Now, get away from here, and leave me alone."

"But this is a special recipe," Mr. Dudley said. "Samantha's won lots of Blue Ribbons with this, hasn't she, John?"

"Mr. Dudley, would you just please go on about your business?" John said. "These men have a job to do, now let them do it."

"Well, all right," Mr. Dudley said. "Mr. Peterson, next time you come to Oregon City, we'll have you over for supper. You'll see, good food never tasted so good."

Mr. Peterson helped Pauline mount the horse, and the three of them rode away. John took advantage of that, and ducked into the General Merchandise Store. When Mr. Dudley looked around, no one was there. He placed the empty pie pan under his arm, began whistling a tune, and went back toward his home.

When John knew Mr. Dudley was out of sight, he returned to his office. He saw that Willie had picked up mail from his trip to Mt. Hood. John saw the Boston newspaper, and sat down to read. Both he and Martha considered the newspaper a vital link with home, and they always devoured every word. It was at such times when he realized how much he actually missed Boston. They were so happy with life in Oregon City, yet it was simply human nature to miss that part of their lives. Perhaps in another year or two, they could return to Boston for a visit.

John was completely absorbed in the newspaper, and didn't hear a thing. He was suddenly aware of someone standing in front of his desk. Looking up, John saw his Indian friend, Little Deer.

"Hello, my friend," Little Deer said. "I am glad to see you."

They talked of their families, and the good harvest last fall. It was soon apparent that Little Deer had something serious to discuss.

"Well, my friend," John said. "What brings you to Oregon City?"

"My father, Chief Black Hawk wishes to speak to you," he said. "Can you come to our village?"

"Yes, of course, I'll come," John said. "Is anything wrong?"

"Yes," he said. "My people signed a treaty with your government, and the white man has broken it. I told my father that you are a good lawyer, and you will help us."

"What kind of treaty was it?" John said.

"Our people sold some land to your government, but now, they refuse to pay us," Little Deer said. "Now they come back to our village, and want more land. They came with guns, and scared our women and children. Can you help us, John? My father will pay you."

"I'll do everything I can," John said. "But I would never expect your people to pay me."

"My father is a proud man, John," he said. "He will never accept something for nothing. You must take his gifts, whatever they may be."

John nodded in agreement, and asked when Chief Black Hawk would like to see him.

"He wants you to come now, John," Little Deer said.

"We can go tomorrow," John said. "Is Morning Dove with you?"

"No. She is too great with child to travel," he said. "She would like Martha to come with you."

"Martha would love to come," John said. Morning Dove and Martha were very close friends, and it pleased him. John remembered the first time Martha saw an Indian. The wagon train was still in the Kansas prairie. At first, Martha was terrified. But Malindy calmed her down, and taught her how to bargain and trade with them. Then she met Morning Dove. It was an instant bond of friendship, love and respect. With all his heart, John wished the white man would find such a bond with all the Indians. He knew the hearts of many white men coveted the good hunting grounds and villages, and sooner or later, there would be trouble. He invited Little Deer to stay at Possum Hollow tonight, and the invitation was joyfully accepted.

At noon, John and Little Deer went to Carolyn's Boarding House and Cafe. The only topic of conversation was the baby.

Little Deer remembered something.

"There was a man not far from our village whose wife died," he said. "Some of our braves saw him with baby."

35

"Do you know his name?" James asked.

Little Deer shook his head no.

"Then we're right back where we started," John said.

The children squealed with delight as they greeted Little Deer. He fashioned a bow for Johnny from a small sapling. He used the slick green bark for the bow string, and shaped another small branch into an arrow. Little Deer taught him how to aim at a target. Soon little arrows were flying around the cabin. Martha ushered them outside, and returned to her kitchen.

"Morning Dove wants you and children to come to our village," Little Deer said. "You are first white woman she ever met, and she honors you greatly."

Martha was humbled by his comment. She felt she'd done nothing worthy of honor, but she loved and cherished her friend.

The March wind was strong and cold as they approached Little Deer's village. A welcome committee of barking dogs and laughing children hailed them. Little Deer greeted his son with a smile, and a new beaver hide. The children began playing with Johnny.

"My father will see you tonight, John," Little Deer said. "Come. I will show you where you stay."

Martha gasped, as she realized he was leading them to a teepee. She wanted to scream.

"Don't you dare say a word," John said. "This time, I agree with you. But we can't refuse this. These people are very precious, and we must do all we can to help them."

She knew he was right, and she would never dream of hurting them. But that Old World upbringing and urbane Boston attitude were fighting for control of Martha again. Suddenly, she saw the humor.

"If Mother and Father could see us now," she said.

John laughed so hard he thought he might fall out of the wagon. He turned his face so the old men of the village couldn't see him laughing. Finally, he regained his composure.

"You will stay here," Little Deer said proudly. "All important people stay here when they come to our village."

He opened the teepee, and escorted them in. A young Indian maiden arose to greet them.

"This is Pretty Star," Little Deer said. "She will bring you food, and help with babies. Pretty Star is my cousin."

She curtsied gracefully, and said, "I help you feed children."

Martha was astonished by the young girl's beauty and charm, and another friendship began.

"Come, John. I will show you our village," Little Deer said.

Pretty Star and Martha attended to Carolyn and Johnny. Soon they were talking and laughing like old friends.

The evening meal was served in Little Deer's teepee. Little Deer had made a papoose cradle, complete with backpack harness, and Morning Dove presented it to Martha.

"Now you carry baby like Indian," Morning Dove said.

"Thank you," Martha replied. "This is so pretty."

At the appointed time, Little Deer escorted John to the tribal counsel. They sat on the ground in a semi-circle, with Chief Black Hawk facing them. At first, John sat comfortably, Indian fashion. But in a few minutes, his legs began to cramp. The pain became so intense that John feared he'd have to get up.

"Be still, my friend," Little Deer said. "You will be all right." He showed John how to balance his weight more evenly, and that relieved the pain.

When the counsel meeting began, Chief Black Hawk arose, and called for the papers. John was in awe of this man. The six foot six chief was in ceremonial dress, and such an intriguing man. But he could not speak English well enough to converse with a white man. Little Deer served as interpreter.

John studied the documents carefully for several minutes. He asked Little Deer some questions, and Little Deer repeated his fathers' answers. This was a legal binding sale of Indian land to the U.S. Government. John could see no reason for them to withhold payment.

"Did anyone ever tell your father why the government doesn't want to pay for this land?" John asked. He thought he could guess the answer, and he was right.

"They told my father they didn't have to pay *savages,*" Little Deer said.

John wondered just which side was the actual savage. He knew many people would think he was betraying the white man's cause. But he couldn't put aside his intense feeling on this subject.

"Tell your father I will do everything I can," he said. "I can't promise anything, but I will try."

Little Deer relayed John's message, waited for Black Hawk's reply, and turned back to John.

"We understand," Little Deer said. "I told my father you are not Medicine Man. All he asks is that you try."

Black Hawk stood up, and looked to his counsel members. Each man gave the chief a sign of approval. One man got up, and went outside. He returned with the Peace Pipe, and gave it to Black Hawk.

"This is our Peace Pipe," Little Deer said. "My father will be the first one to smoke. Then he will pass it to the others. Finally, it will come to me, then to you."

John knew this ceremony was the tribes official seal or approval and trust in him.

"It smells very strong," John said. "What's in it?"

"You may not want to know, my friend," Little Deer said.

Martha couldn't remember when she'd had such a wonderful evening. The children laughed and played together, wrestling as all little boys do, and Carolyn slept peacefully.

Martha thought about the empty shallowness of those grand parties she'd attended in Boston. She'd stood in a receiving line with a glass of champaign she couldn't stand, and smiled at obnoxious people she detested until she almost became ill. Martha knew many of those people felt the same way she did. Some of those ladies in their finest evening gowns were miserable, unhappy, and very lonely. Yet, they glued a smile on their faces and went through this disgusting ritual once a month, because they had married the money, not the man. Now their duty forced them to dance to a tune they hadn't bargained for, but couldn't refuse.

Of course, not all of them were unhappy. Mary Baxter Fuller seemed deliriously happy. Why shouldn't she be happy? Her father was a U.S. Senator, her brother was a celebrated artist, and her husband, Captain Martin Fuller, was an Army officer, and government surveyor. They were indeed happy, and well suited to each other. Martha recalled several other couples she knew were happy. But there was too much contrast between her attitudes in Boston and her attitudes now. She wondered if people in this village ever struggled with such social questions.

Morning Dove gave an anguished cry.

"Are you all right, dear?" Martha asked.

"My baby comes," she said.

"I will get Old Woman," Pretty Star said.

"No, there is no time," Morning Dove said. "Help me lay down."

Martha and Pretty Star helped her to the buffalo robe on the floor.

"You must help me, Martha," she said.

"But...but...I don't know what to do," Martha said.

There wasn't time to plan or think, as the baby's head appeared. Martha knew the pain Morning Dove felt, though her friend never uttered another word. The next thing Martha knew, she was holding a beautiful Indian Princess. They laughed and cried, as Pretty Star cut the umbilical cord, and spanked the tiny little girl. Air rushed into her lungs, and Rose began to cry.

"Little Deer said to call her Rose," Morning Dove said. "He said a rose is a pretty red flower white woman likes."

"She's more beautiful than a million roses," Martha said.

Outside, the men heard the cries of the newborn infant. Little Deer looked at John, then at his father.

"Go, my son," Black Hawk said.

"John, I can't even begin to describe this night," Martha said. "There are not enough words on earth to explain it."

"And I thought I was the one always looking for adventure," John said. "Wait till Malindy hears about this."

"John, you wouldn't."

"Yes, I will, if you don't stop talking and let me sleep."

John and Martha were awakened by the noise of the busy Indian village. At first, they were both disoriented, and frightened. Martha gathered her children between herself and John. A moment later, Pretty Star opened the teepee.

"Come, quickly," she said.

"What's wrong?" John said.

"You'll see," Pretty Star said. "Chief Black Hawk tell you."

John and Martha couldn't imagine what might be wrong. They dressed, and John went outside. Pretty Star led John to the Chief's teepee, where Little Deer greeted them. John could tell by his friend's expression that it was bad news.

"What's wrong? John said.

"Dr. Whitman, he is dead."

John felt the weakness in his knees and legs. Dr. Marcus Whitman had established a mission to the Indians, and encouraged the wagon trains as they came near his mission.

All John could say was, "When and how?"

"My father will tell you," Little Deer said.

They went inside, and Chief Black Hawk motioned for them to set down. Little Deer told John all that his father said.

"White man's disease made Cayuse children sick. Medicine Man didn't know what to do. Dr. Whitman help white children, and they live. He tell Indian to do same things white man's children do. But all Indian children die, white children live. Cayuse raiding party went to mission, kill Dr. Whitman, his wife and child."

Little Deer stopped, and tears ran down his face. John began to cry.

"Did anyone survive?" John said.

Chief Black Hawk spoke again, and Little Deer repeated it to John.

"Cayuse kill fifteen, some escaped," Little Deer said.

"Was it Mary Ann Bridger, Jim Bridgers's daughter?"

"She died later," Little Deer said. "Some may come to your village, John."

John was stunned. He had met Dr. Whitman in Boston, and again when the wagon train came close to his mission. John respected him.

"When did this happen?" John said.

Little Deer asked his father.

"It was before first snow," Little Deer said.

"That would be late November," John said.

Chief Black Hawk stood up, and motioned for Little Deer and John to leave. They walked back to the teepee.

"I will see you again, my friend," Little Deer said. "My father wants to honor you tonight."

"Tell your father I honor him," John said.

John told Martha, and they wept together

"Dr. Whitman was a good man," John said.

They went about the day with heavy hearts. Pretty Star helped Martha with the children, and coached her on tonight's ceremony.

John and Little Deer prepared for tonight's ceremony. John admitted he was nervous, but Little Deer calmed his fears.

"Don't worry, my friend," Little Deer said. He helped John with the ceremonial paint, and made sure everything was just right.

Martha wanted to laugh when John returned. His chest and face were painted with the special pigments, and she wondered if this was really John.

"Yes, it's really me," he said. Johnny loved it, and Carolyn wanted to eat the paint.

The ceremony seemed to drag on, and John grew tired. Martha and Pretty Star finished their meal, and let the children play til they fell asleep.

"Come, my friend," Little Deer said. "You dance with us."

John started to protest that he didn't know how, but Little Deer motioned him forward. He watched the other young braves for a moment, and picked up the rhythm of the dance. Slow, and unsure of himself, John took a few steps. Gradually, he relaxed, and began to enjoy the ritual. By the time the dance ended, John was exhausted.

All the young braves seemed happy with John, and Chief Black Hawk gave his approval.

"My father says you are one with us, my friend," Little Deer said.

"Tell you father I am honored," John said. "What does this dance mean, anyway?"

Little Deer explained to his father, then to John.

"You are our friend, John Campbell," he said. "My people are your friends. You help us, we help you."

Martha watched in astonishment. A million thoughts ran through her mind. *I can't believe this is happening* she thought. *I can't wait to tell Father and Adam.* She laughed at that last thought. *All of Boston will go crazy when they hear about this.*

John returned to her side, and explained the significance of the ceremony. She also felt honored to be called a friend of these people.

John formed a plan to get payment for sale of the Indian property. He knew this would tax his legal skills, but that was all right. This was the right thing to do, and he was glad to be a part of it.

The next morning, John and Martha got the children ready for the trip back home. They said good bye to Little Deer and his family.

"He just beams with pride for that little girl," John said, as they left the village.

Martha felt blessed to have been part of all that had transpired last night.

4 THE SCHOOL

While John prepared his brief on the sale of Indian land for the Provisional Government Office, Martha prepared Becky and Jenny for the Oregon Institute. She needed to visit the campus, and get the general atmosphere of the school. The girls needed the enrollment guidelines, courses available, tuition and books, and a host of other things. Martha carefully wrote out a list of things she needed. She would ask Becky and Jenny to accompany her. The trip itself would be educational for them.

They chose Wednesday as their day of travel. John would go to the Provisional Government Office, while Martha and the children went to the Oregon Institute.

John knocked on Mr. Meeker's door.

"Hello, John," Mr. Meeker said. "It's good to see you again. Can I help you with something?"

"Hello, sir," John said. "And yes, I do need your help with a matter."

"Well, John, set down, and let's talk about it."

45

John showed him the sale papers. Mr. Meeker studied them for a moment, then got out the copies that were given to him.

"Why, there's no mention of a price in my copies," Mr. Meeker said. "What they gave me says the land was given to them. Now, that really makes me mad. What's he trying to do, rob people?"

"I was afraid of that," John said. "Is there anything we can do? They owe Chief Black Hawk a lot of money. I'd like to show them that not every white man is bad."

Mr. Meeker thought for a moment. "By golly, John. I believe we can do something. Let me find Mr. Peterson, and we'll get this snake, and put him in jail"

"Can we make him pay for the land?" John said.

"We'll make him pay every penny of it," he said. "Come with me, John. Let's show Mr. Peterson your papers."

Mr. Peterson was setting the linotype on his printing press when they arrived. He had spilled a small puddle of printers ink on the floor, and cautioned them to step over it. They shook hands.

"I hope you didn't bring any of those confounded apple pies, did you?" he asked John.

"No, sir," John said. "Mr. Dudley doesn't even know I'm here."

"Thank God for small favors," he said. "Now, how can I help you gentlemen?"

John and Mr. Meeker related the facts of the Indian land sale, and showed him the two sets of papers.

"Do you know this Mr. Mason?" Mr. Meeker said.

"I know of him," Mr. Peterson said. "This is not the first complaint I've heard on him. Should we bring him in here, and confront him?"

"Yes, I think we should," Mr. Meeker said. "You say he's done things like this before?"

"Well, he bought a piece of land up around the new town of Portland," Mr. Peterson said. "There was a great big argument about the price, and I don't think he ever paid the full amount."

"Then let's talk to Dr. McLoughlin, and see if we can force him to pay up on both of these things," Mr. Meeker said.

They talked to Dr. McLoughlin, and he agreed with their plan. But they would also need the cooperation of Mr. Horton in Portland.

"This may take a couple of days," Dr. McLoughlin said. "But don't worry, we'll get the money for Chief Black Hawk. I'll send Peterson down to Oregon City with the money for the Chief."

John felt relieved as he started home. He would have good news for Little Deer and his people. Every time he was able to help someone, he felt his life was worthwhile. *It took a long time for me to learn that, but I guess better late than never* he thought.

Martha enjoyed the ride to the Oregon Institute. Becky and Jenny played with the children, and that kept them occupied and happy. She remembered when she'd entered a new school for the first time, especially in Paris. She'd felt alone, and homesick. Martha loved the French language, and the rich social history of Paris. But that didn't comfort her. If there had been someone she knew, a relative, or a friend to share the experience, her studies would have been much better. Martha was glad that Jenny and Becky could share this experience together.

The school was a three story wooden building, towering above the other buildings in town. On the front lawn was the sign *Oregon Institute,* and below that was the school's motto, *not unto ourselves alone are we born.* The school was founded in 1842, by missionary Jason Lee. It served to educate the missionary children, Indian children, and now served the higher educational needs of new settlers.

Becky and Jenny looked at the building in awe. Martha sighed, took the girls by their hands, and said, "Come on, girls. Let's go inside."

They walked to the end of the hallway. It was an eerie quietness, and their footsteps echoed through the building. To the left were classrooms, and the office was the first door on the right. Martha walked to the door, and knocked.

"Come in," he said.

"Hello, sir. I'm Martha Campbell, and this is Becky and Jenny Miller. We'd like some information on enrollment, please."

"Hello, ladies," he said, shaking their hands. "My name is David Smith, and I teach history here. I'm filling in for Mr. Strong. He's our Administrator, and he's out sick this week." He pulled out three chairs, and they all sat down.

"So, you ladies would like to enroll. Let me see, I think he keeps those papers over here." He got up, and looked through a big wooden file cabinet. "Yes, here they are." He pulled out three sets.

"Oh, no, sir," Martha said. "I don't need to enroll. I graduated many years ago. My friends, Becky and Jenny are interested in college."

"Oh, I'm sorry," he said. "Please excuse me. Here we are, girls." He handed them the papers.

"Sir, maybe I should have a copy of those papers," Martha said. He handed them to her.

"And here are the prerequisites, financial needs, and a list of the studies we offer," he said. "I'm sure you'll find all the information you need."

"Thank you," Martha said. "May we take them home, and consider this?"

"Certainly," he said. "Would you ladies like to tour our building? I'd be delighted to show you everything about our school."

"Yes," Martha said. "That would be very helpful."

They walked down the hall, and Mr. Smith explained each classroom on the first floor. At the other end of the hall were the stairs to the second floor. The steps felt rather weak, and seemed to sag a little as they walked. The entire staircase squeaked and groaned, and the noise seemed extra loud.

"Ladies, do you have any questions? Mr. Smith said.

"If we decide to do this, when can we start?" Becky said.

"Our next class will enroll this fall," Mr. Smith said. "All the information you need is in the papers I've given you. Are we ready for the third floor?"

Martha wondered about the safety of the stairs leading to the third floor, but didn't want to dampen their enthusiasm. Their excitement was contagious, and Martha felt good about this.

At the conclusion of the tour, Becky and Jenny began looking through the information they'd been given. Martha caught the gleam in their eyes.

"Oh, Martha, this is so wonderful," Becky said.

"I can't wait to get started," Jenny said.

"Read this information very carefully, girls," Martha said.

"We can't afford to pay for any of this," Jenny said.

"I think I can get you both scholarship grants," Martha said. "Just let me take care of that, and don't worry about it."

"But how can we ever repay you?" Becky said. "Besides, you don't even have to do this, Martha."

"Repay me by being the best students you can possibly be," she said. "And, no, I don't have to do it, but I want to do this. Your entire family has been so good to us, and this is just a small way of returning that kindness to you."

They talked and planned all the way home. Martha was just as excited as the girls were.

"It's almost like I'm starting school again," Martha said. "But girls, we have a lot to do now. We have to decide what subjects you'll study. I'll come by Friday evening, and we'll go through all this material together."

Martha and the girls arrived back home just before sundown. Martha drove the wagon to the Boarding House, and said good night to them. She was anxious to get home. There was so much she wanted to tell John.

Martha built the fire in the fireplace. She remembered the many times on the wagon train when Malindy helped her with this chore. She went down to the spring, and found the jars of milk she'd put there to keep cool. On the way back to the house, she gathered eggs from the hen house. Martha placed the eggs in her apron pocket, taking care not to break them. Once she got back inside, she began preparing the meal.

John was anxious to tell Martha of his successful trip. He was also hungry, and as he drove into the yard, he could smell the wonderful aroma of fresh baked biscuits. *I'm so hungry I could even eat one of Mrs. Dudley's pies* he thought.

5 THE INTERVIEW

John welcomed Mr. Peterson into his office. He knew Peterson was bringing the money for Chief Black Hawk, but didn't expect to see him so soon.

"John, this is Mr. Arthur Kelly," Mr. Peterson said. "He's a reporter from Boston, and he'd like to do a story on you."

"Hello, John," he said. "I hear you're an exceptional attorney. I'd like to ride with you to this Indian village, if I may."

"Yes," John said. "What newspaper are you with? I'm from Boston, and we always look forward to reading everything about home."

"I'm with the **Boston News Letter**," he said. "I'd like to get some background on you and your family. What my editor would really like is more about this Indian land deal."

"John, I have the money for Chief Black Hawk," Mr. Peterson said. "I have to get back home today, so here is the money."

He gave John a bulging saddlebag, and said, "Count this. And if you'll write a receipt, I'll be on my way."

John opened the saddlebag, and began counting.

"Mr. Kelly, you know where to find me, and good luck," Peterson said.

"The money is correct," John said. He wrote out the receipt, and Mr. Peterson thanked him.

"I'll see you in a few days, Kelly," he said. "Thanks again, John."

"Tell me a little about yourself, John," Mr. Kelly said. "And, please call me Arthur."

"Well, Arthur, my wife and I were born in Boston, and our families are still there," John said.

"Yes. I saw your name on The Oregon Emigration Society," Arthur said. "I believe your father is Adam Campbell. Is that correct?"

Oh, no. Not this again John thought. "Yes, he's my father. And Charles Montgomery is my wife's father."

"I'd like to know why you gave up such a lucrative private practice, John," he said. "You couldn't possibly make money *here.*"

"I make a very good living here," John said. "In the last few years, I've learned that money isn't everything, Arthur. I was very unhappy in Boston, but here, I'm the happiest man in the world."

They talked extensively about Boston, Oregon City, and the recent Indian land sale. They ate lunch at Carolyn's Boarding House and Café, and John introduced him to James and Carolyn.

"Well, Arthur, let's take this money to Chief Black Hawk," John said. John almost wished Arthur hadn't come here. Yet, he liked Arthur, and it

53

was always good to hear about home. But as sure as his story was printed, John knew just how Adam and Charles would react.

They continued their conversation until they reached the Indian village. They were greeted by a group of children. John saw Little Deer walking toward them. He introduced Little Deer to Arthur, and they went to see Chief Black Hawk.

Little Deer explained to his father as John gave the money to him. The Chief's eyes met John's, and his face softened.

"My father thanks you, John," Little Deer said. "You are real friend to our people."

A smile came to the Chief's face, as he shook John's hand.

"John, would they mind if I stayed here a few days, and do a story on them?" Arthur said.

Little Deer asked his father, and the Chief nodded his approval.

"I can find my way back to Oregon City, John," he said. "I'll see you in a few days."

John drove the buggy back to his office. *I wouldn't trade what we have now for all the money in Boston* he thought. He began reviewing the notes for his next case, and formed the strategy he would use. He felt happy, and satisfied.

Martha had spent the entire day reading the information from the Oregon Institute. She just couldn't see a way around it–the girls would have to learn Latin as a prerequisite. *How am I ever going to get this through to them?* she thought. *Their English is still from the backwoods of Kentucky. And I haven't even thought of Latin in many years.*

She found her old text books from New York, and began looking through them. She would use these to teach the extra things they needed in math, English, history, and philosophy. But they would also need French, Latin and art.

"I think those books are out in the barn," she told Johnny. "When your father gets home, I'll have him bring those in."

Martha had been so caught up in her teaching plans that she didn't realize John would be home in a few minutes.

They talked through their evening meal, each sharing all the events of the day. Martha was pleased to hear they'd paid Chief Black Hawk.

"Now, don't be surprised to meet a reporter from the **Boston News Letter**," John said. "His name is Arthur Kelly. He knows Charles and my father. I got the impression he's out here at their suggestion, even though the paper is sponsoring this. He met James and Carolyn today, and went with me to the Indian village."

"I had hoped that Father would understand by now," Martha said. There was a touch of sadness in her remark, for she longed to have her father's love and acceptance. "What shall I tell him?"

"He seems to be a nice chap. Just be honest, and tell what you're comfortable revealing," John said.

Martha took her children with her as she went to school. This would be the first day of classes, and she was as excited as the students.

The school week passed by rapidly. The children were well behaved, and all of them seemed to catch on with ease. She loved teaching them, watching their faces light up when they understood the concept she'd explained. She always felt that she learned the most, as Life had many new things to teach her each day.

Martha stopped by for a visit with Carolyn and James.

"I see no one has claimed the baby yet," Martha said.

"I'm beginning to think we'll have to raise her ourselves," James said. "But that's all right, cause I don't think either of us could stand it without her, now."

Martha squeezed his hand, and smiled.

Willie's taxi pulled up to the Boarding House. Becky, Jenny and Mr. Johnson got out and paid Willie. He came inside for a moment to hug Carolyn, and eat a quick bite. Then he was off again.

"Girls, we have a lot of work to do," Martha said. "Are you ready?"

"I guess so," Becky said.

Martha decided to give them a general outline first. She explained the need for higher understanding of math, English and history. She loaned them her old textbooks, showing them examples, and briefly explaining why it was necessary.

Then she told them about Latin. They seemed puzzled.

"But if nobody talks in Latin anymore, why do we have to learn it?" Jenny said.

Martha explained a little more to them. "Many universities feel that Latin trains the mind to think precisely and quickly," she said. "Many of our English words have their roots in Latin. It's really a beautiful language."

"Did you have to learn this when you went to school?" Jenny asked.

"Yes, I did," Martha said. "I also learned French, and some Spanish. Later on, you'll learn about the classic literature in Latin. But for now, let's take it one thing at a time."

She gave them assignments in English, math, history, and beginning Latin. "Now, next Friday, we'll go over all this. If there's anything you don't understand, please let me know." She said good night to them, and left for home.

When Martha and the children arrived at Possum Hollow, she noticed that John was home early. When they went inside, she saw that they had company. She didn't know this man, but assumed him to be Arthur Kelly.

John made the proper introductions. Martha observed the love and pride in his face as he presented the children to Arthur. John excused himself, and began his evening work.

"Mrs. Campbell, I'd like to ask you a few questions, while you cook," Arthur said.

"Sure," Martha said. She began preparing the dough for Malindy's favorite biscuits.

"I understand that you never wanted to come to Oregon," he said. "But now that you're here, have your opinions changed?"

"It's true that I didn't want to come," Martha said. "My life is so different now, and I can't imagine ever living in Boston again. The trip out here opened my eyes to so many things."

"Ah, yes," Arthur said. "Tell me about the wagon train to Oregon."

"That trip took six months," Martha said. She recalled leaving Boston, the train rides to Chicago, and the stagecoach's to St. Louis.

She told of meeting Calvin and Malindy. "These biscuits I'm cooking now are from her favorite recipe," she said. One by one, she described the people and events of that astonishing journey.

"Dr. McLoughlin told me that you teach school here in Oregon City," Arthur said. "I can tell that you're a woman of education and culture. Aren't your considerable abilities withering away here in this boorish wasteland?"

"*Au contraire*," Martha said. "In fact, this is the place where my 'abilities' are most needed." As they ate, Martha recounted how she'd not only taught the children, but helped many adults to see the need for a good education. She felt her crowning jewel was helping Becky and Jenny Miller to prepare for the Oregon Institute.

"You mean these unlettered girls are thinking of attending an institution of higher learning?" Arthur said. "What school would ever accept them?"

"Mr. Kelly," Martha snapped. "They are not 'unlettered.' You should contact the Oregon Institute. And don't you ever insult me or any of my students again. If you have no further questions, this interview is finished, and you are excused from the table. Good night."

Kelly was shocked. He was not accustomed to strong willed women. He started to get up.

"Mr. Kelly, wait," Martha said. "I'm sorry. I shouldn't have said that. But I get very defensive about my students, especially when I'm so close to them. Please, let's continue the interview."

John couldn't control the laughter, and turned his head, coughing into his napkin. When he regained his composure, he broke the tension.

"Arthur met Little Deer the other day," he said to Martha.

"Did you meet his wife, Morning Dove?" Martha said. "She is one of my closest friends, and so beautiful. I must find out her beauty secrets."

Arthur took out a large briefcase, and displayed his illustrations of the Indian village. The pencil drawings were exquisite of Chief Black Hawk, Little Deer, Morning Dove and their children, and all the tribal council. There was one of Little Deer setting majestically on his horse. John gasped at its beauty.

"Here, John," Arthur said. "Little Deer is your friend, and you should have this." He gave it to John, then took out many more sketches. He gave some of Morning Dove, Little Deer, and the children to Martha.

"I want to get some drawings of you and your family, John," he said. "Martha, I hope you don't think I'm intruding, but I want some of your class, also."

Martha was very pleased. "Yes, I'd like that," she said.

After the meal, Martha cleared the table, and washed her dishes. John read a story to his children from the Bible

Arthur took out his pencil, and began to draw. "That looks like a very old Bible, John," he said.

"It is very old," John said. "It belonged to my grandfather. When we left Boston, I asked my father if I could have it. He never wanted anything to do with religion, and was probably glad to get rid of it. Someday, Johnny with have this."

They talked late into the night, and John and Martha revealed their deepest feelings about many things.

The children slept with John and Martha, and Arthur occupied the other bedroom. As Martha slipped into bed, she felt the bed shaking. She realized John was laughing.

"What's so funny?" she whispered.

"The way you tried to end the interview," he whispered. "Didn't you see his face? He probably thought you'd chase him with that big carving knife on the table."

"Oh, just shut up, and go to sleep, before you wake up these children." He continued to laugh, as Martha sighed in disgust.

Martha had been planning the lessons all week. She hoped the girls were well prepared, for she knew she had to be tough on them. Without her guidance, and their own self-discipline, this would be impossible. Then there was the unexpected problem of Charles Price. He didn't want Jenny to attend the Oregon Institute. He seemed to think that if she had more knowledge than he possessed, it constituted an attack on his manhood.

Martha got her wagon ready, and went to Carolyn's Boarding House. She had no choice but to bring along Johnny and Carolyn, too. She secured their promises of good behavior. She'd planned an hour session each with Jenny and Becky.

"Hello, James," Martha said. She hugged Carolyn, and played with the baby for a while. "No word on who the parents might be?"

"No," Carolyn said. "Mr. Meeker said if nobody claims her by the end of the year, we can adopt her. That's what we want to do, Martha. What do you think?"

"I think that's wonderful," Martha said. "I can't think of better parents. As Malindy says, she's 'fell into good hands' here."

Martha held the baby for a moment. "She sure is a good little girl. Can you watch my two while I help Jenny and Becky?"

"Sure, we can," Carolyn said. "But Jenny and Becky haven't got home yet. They'll be here in a little while."

Becky and Billy Joe came home first.

"Martha, I need to talk to you," Becky said. They sat down at Carolyn's long kitchen table, and Billy Joe took Carolyn. Johnny went with James to collect the eggs.

"Martha, that Charles is impossible," she said.

I was afraid of that Martha thought. "Oh? What's he done?" she said.

"Well, he don't want Jenny to study, and he won't help her, either," Becky said. "Last night, they had a really bad fight about this. It'll break her heart if she has to stop learning."

"I'll talk to him," Martha said. "But I can't promise anything."

"He's real stubborn about this," Becky said.

Jenny and Charles came in. He seemed to be agitated.

"Hi, Martha," Jenny said.

"Martha, if you're here to fill her head with all your crazy ideas, well, you can just forget it," Charles said.

"Charles, we can work something out," Martha said.

"You bet we can," he said. "She ain't doing this."

"Charles, no. Don't act like this," Jenny said.

"What do you think I am, woman?" he shouted. "I can't pay for none of this. And you can't either. Where we gonna get the money?"

"I'll get scholarships for Becky and Jenny," Martha said.

"We don't want no handouts," he said.

"That's not a handout," Martha said. She saw that trying to reason with him was impossible.

"Come on, Jenny," Charles said. "Let's go."

"No, Charles," Jenny said. "I want to learn. Why can't you understand that?" Tears ran down her face.

"Well, what good did it ever do me?" he said. "I went plumb through all eight grades, and what did it get me—nothing. All I ever do is follow a stupid old plow mule all day, dragging logs up out of the woods. Them logs makes somebody else rich. But all I ever get is just a few dollars. I can't even get ahead enough to build my own house for me and you. Now you're gonna run off to that Oregon Institute. What about me, Jenny? Where do I fit in, now?"

Charles stalked out, and slammed the door as he left.

"Why can't he understand?" Jenny said. "I ain't trying to be smarter than he is. I ain't trying to take over. My whole life, people have made fun of us, cause we come from Kentucky, and don't have much education. But I want to know things, and I aim to know, whether he likes it, or not."

"Are you sure, Jenny?" Martha said. "Sometimes we have to pay a very high price for things we want."

"Yes, I'm sure," she said.

They went to Becky's room for tonight's study.

"Martha, can I listen in?" Billy Joe said.

"Well, of course you can," Martha said.

They struggled with the more advanced math, and Becky's spelling was atrocious. But the most difficult lessons were Latin. Even Martha was having trouble with it. Finally they did manage to construct a sentence in Latin. Martha was proud of them.

"Girls, next week, we'll do another sentence in Latin," Martha said. "And we'll get started in Philosophy." She gave them reading assignments, and told Billy Joe to read it, too.

6 LAW AND ORDER

Martha introduced Arthur Kelly to her class.

"He'll be in our class today, drawing pictures of us, and listening to us," Martha said. "So I want all of you to be on your best behavior. Can you do that for me?"

"Yes," they said in unison.

Arthur smiled, and waved to the class. He sat down up front, and began to draw. As he finished a sketch, he'd hold it up for the class to see. The children liked Arthur, and enjoyed his company.

Out of the corner of his eye, Arthur saw something. He thought he saw a man with a gun walk past the window, and disappear into the shadows. Arthur reminded himself that this was the frontier, and many law abiding citizens carried guns. He dismissed the incident, and decided not to mention it.

Arthur captured the children's spelling contest, and their tug-of-war at recess.

"Martha, do you miss Boston?" Arthur said.

"Yes," she said. "I miss my parents and friends. Before we left Independence on the wagon train, I would cry for all those I left behind. But then I realized that life goes on, and I began to enjoy my life more than I ever had."

"Would you like to go back to Boston?"

"Yes," she said. "But just for a visit. I don't want to live there anymore. In Boston, I took too many things for granted, and my priorities were out of balance. Once I got those things in perspective, I'm very happy here."

Martha's class had delighted Arthur, and it was easy to draw and write. He found himself wishing the day was longer. Arthur headed for Carolyn's Boarding House. Martha always picked up her children at the boarding house. She took Johnny's hand, and carried the baby, as they walked to John's office.

Willie's carriage came to a sudden stop in front of John's office. All that dust and dirt seemed to drift right inside, and settled on the children's clothes. It had been hot and dry for the past week, and Martha knew that wasn't Willie's fault. But she wished he'd be a little more concerned about stirring up the dust.

Willie jumped off the carriage, and ran into John's office.

"Where's John?" he said. Without waiting for Martha's reply, he continued. "Martha, I know you remember that Ezra Hill that was on the wagon train." He paused to catch his breath.

"Yes," she said. "I sure do. How could any of us forget him?"

"Well, he's here," Willie said. "I just seen him a while ago. I know it's him. Where's John?"

"I think he went out to see Mr. Wilson today," Martha said. "He should be back pretty soon. Did you tell Big Jim?"

"Not yet," Willie said. "But I guess I better go tell him." He got back on his carriage, and went to the Sheriff's office.

The quiet peace of Oregon City had been broken.

Oh, no. We don't need this Martha thought.

Willie ran into Big Jim's office.

"Jim," he said. "Ezra Hill is here. I seen him."

"Whoa, Willie," Jim said. "What are you talking about?"

"Ezra Hill, that man on the wagon train, that had his arm cut off at Fort Laramie," Willie said.

"Did he do something bad?"

"I don't know, Jim," Willie said. "But I thought you ought to know he's here."

"Well, I'm glad you told me, Willie," Jim said. "But if he ain't done nothing yet, then it ain't wrong for him to be here. But I'll watch out for him. He just might be mad at me for turning him over to Fort Laramie. Let me know if you hear anything."

John returned to his office. He played with the children, then Martha told him of Arthur's visit to her class.

"There's something else, too," Martha said. "Ezra Hill is here. Willie saw him."

"Does Jim know?"

"Willie was going to tell him."

"Well, let's just hope he doesn't try to get even," John said. "Let's get home to Possum Hollow. I'm hungry." John got some law books, and plenty of paper for his notes. He carried Carolyn, and Martha took Johnny to the wagon.

Ezra Hill carried a grudge against Big Jim, and everyone else in the world. It seemed he'd been angry all his life. He'd even admit he didn't always know why he was so angry, but that raging fury was constantly there. As an outlaw, his reputation often proceeded his arrival into any community. Sometimes, he wanted it that way. He wanted Big Jim to worry about where he was, and what he wanted. Ezra had lost his shooting arm. He was naturally left handed, and learning to shoot with his right hand had been very difficult. He'd settle the score later with a certain doctor who amputated his arm. Right now, he wanted to take care of the one who sent him to the doctor at Fort Laramie.

He pushed the barroom door open, and stomped up to the bar. No one paid any attention to him. It always made him mad when no one acknowledged him.

"Whiskey," he growled at the bar tender.

"Haven't seen you around here before," the bar tender said. "What's your name?"

Ezra drank the shot of whiskey, and wanted more. The bar tender poured him another drink. Ezra grabbed the bottle.

"It don't make you no never mind what my name is," Ezra said. "You know a man named Jim Cross, used to be a wagon scout?"

"Why, yes," the bar tender said. "He's the Sheriff here. Mighty fine man."

"Huh," Ezra murmured. "Ain't nothing fine about him."

"Maybe it ain't none of my business, Mister," the bar tender said. "But we've got a nice, peaceful place here, and we don't want no trouble. And if you come here to cause trouble, then just move on."

"You're right, bar keep," Ezra said. "It ain't none of your business. And if you think you're big enough, make me move."

"I'm not going to fight you, if that's what you want," the bar tender said. "I'm just telling you how we all feel. There's not a man or woman in this town that wouldn't stand up for Big Jim. You'll have to fight us all to get to him."

"I can handle that," Ezra said. "You just tell Cross that somebody's looking for him. I'll take care of the rest."

He took the bottle of whiskey with him, and stalked out of the bar. Ezra went down to the river front, and spent the night under a friendly tree.

The next morning, Oregon City was buzzing with news about Ezra Hill. Many people had stopped Big Jim on his way into town. They all meant well, and just tried to show their concern and support. But they made him late for work, and had him a little agitated. Helen was upset now.

"Jim, please be careful," she said.

"I'll be all right," he said. "Harry and George will be here. We'll make it just fine."

They stopped at Carolyn's Boarding House. Helen and the children went in, and Big Jim went to see John.

"Morning, John," he said. "I reckon you heard. Everybody else heard about it, too."

"Yes, I heard," John said. "These things spread like wildfire."

"What can I do with him, John? He ain't done nothing, yet," Jim said. "And if I wait till he picks a fight, it might be too late."

"Maybe we'd better talk to Dr. McLoughlin and Mr. Meeker," John said.

Big Jim agreed.

Arthur Kelly walked into John's office.

John introduced him to Big Jim.

"So you're the famous wagon scout," Arthur said. "I'm sure glad to meet you. If you have time today, I'd like to get to know you a little better."

Big Jim nodded.

"Arthur, you may be able to help us out with a bad situation," John said.

John and Big Jim explained about Ezra Hill. Arthur took notes as fast as he could.

"You mean this man has threatened you?" Arthur said.

"Yeah, in a manner of speaking," Big Jim said. "But if I get afraid of every little bully that comes along, I ain't got no business being the sheriff. "

Arthur told them about seeing a man with a gun go past the schoolhouse yesterday.

69

"It was probably Hill," Big Jim said.

"Arthur, could you ride up to the Provisional Government Office, and tell Mr. Meeker about this?" John said.

"Yes. I'd be glad to," he said.

They gave him more details on Ezra Hill, and requested that Mr. Peterson return with him.

"Oh, Sheriff, I'm glad you're all right," Councilman Dudley said. He shook Jim's hand vigorously.

Oh, no John thought. *This is not the time, Councilman.*

"And who are you?" Mr. Dudley asked Arthur.

"Oh, I'm sorry," John said. "Councilman Dudley, this is Arthur Kelly. He's a newspaper reporter from Boston. Arthur, this is one of our city councilmen, Mr. Dudley."

They shook hands, and Mr. Dudley started in.

"Say, you know my wife bakes the best apple pies in the world, doesn't she, John? Anyway, I thought if you could just taste one of her pies, you might give it mention in your paper…"

"Uh, Arthur, we are in a hurry about Mr. Meeker's reply," John said. "You'd better get going."

"Councilman, it's good to meet you. I'm sure I'll see you again before long. Good day, sir." Arthur left the office, and went to inform Mr. Meeker.

"Jim, I'm sure glad you're all right," Mr. Dudley said again. "The wife was worried about you. And she's got a pie ready to eat. I'll bring it down for you."

"Thank you, Mr. Dudley," Jim said. "But she really doesn't have to feed me like that."

"Mr. Dudley," John said. "Why don't you go look up the city statutes on making threats against elected officials? I really need that information today, and I just won't have the time to look it up. Could you do that for me?"

"Why, sure, John," he said. "I'd be glad to help out. Maybe I can get the wife to bake you a pie, too."

Before John could tell him not to bother about the pie, he'd left. But if a pie would keep the good councilman out of the way, it might be worth it.

Ezra Hill shaved and cleaned himself up. He'd spotted Carolyn's Boarding House, and decided that would be a nice place to stay. He opened the door and went inside. Carolyn and James recognized him.

"I should've knowed it was you two," Ezra said. "Got any nice rooms for a few days, real cheap?"

"No, we don't have any," James said. His heart pounded in his chest.

"You're turning me down?" Hill said. "But your sign out there says 'vacancy'. And I thought if you said you had a room, since I'm asking real nice, you'd rent it to me."

"Well, I'm not renting a room to you," James said. "There's another boarding house just on the south end of town. They've got plenty of rooms. They just started up, and they need business."

"And here I thought you was nice Christian folks," he said. "A decent person ain't got a chance anymore." He turned and left.

Helen and Susan came in to see what was going on.

71

"What would he know about decent folks?" Carolyn said.

"Shh," James said. "We sure don't want him coming back here. I got to set down a while." He sat down, and Carolyn brought his some water.

"All right," James said. "Let's all go on with the work. We've got to fix supper for tonight."

"I wonder what happened to Libby?" Carolyn said. "She's not with him. I hope nothing bad happened. I always liked her, and I felt sorry for her."

"Woman, sometimes you'd feel sorry for anybody," James said.

She swatted him with her dish towel, and let his comment go by.

Truth was, Ezra was broke. He'd spent all his money just getting here. His attempt to rent a room from James and Carolyn was mostly for shock effect when he saw who they were. Maybe he could persuade the Livery Stable to let him sleep in their hay loft. If there was a bank in town, he could solve two problems—get rid of the man who caused him to loose his arm, and get enough money to get out of here.

Finding sleeping quarters in the hay wasn't hard. They just wanted him to clean out the stable every day in return for his bed. Getting money from the bank was a much bigger challenge. But he'd done that many times before, and knew he could do it again.

By mid-afternoon, Arthur had returned with Mr. Peterson. They went to see Big Jim.

"Mr. Meeker said to arrest him, if he says one word to you," Mr. Peterson said. "Then we'll transport him up to Portland. What does he look like?"

"Well, he's about six foot tall, dark hair, little thin black moustache, old brown hat. James said he had on a faded red shirt. And his left arm's missing—amputated. I heard he's staying down there at the Livery Stable."

John thought it best to escort Martha and the children home tonight.

"I'd kind of like to know more about him," Martha said. "I thought Major Nelson was sending him back to Texas."

"He probably escaped," John said.

Big Jim didn't like to go back home when potential trouble might be brewing. He sent Helen and the children home, then returned to his office.

"George, Harry, come in here a minute," Big Jim said. George Morris and Harry Eldon were Jim's most trusted deputies. He knew they were good, honest men who couldn't be bought.

"Boys, I wonder if that Ezra Hill ain't gonna try something tonight, or maybe tomorrow night," he said. "George, you've lived with the Indians. See if you can watch him tonight, without him knowing it. Me and Harry'll stay here tonight. Report back to me every two hours or so,"

"Yeah," he said. "I bet he does try something." George got some extra bullets. He pulled off his boots, and put on the soft moccasins. He slipped out the back door, and went around behind the Livery Stable to an empty shed.

Arthur Kelly came by to talk with Big Jim.

"Who is this Ezra Hill, and what has he done?" he said.

Big Jim explained about Ezra's problems on the wagon train.

"We kept smelling something awful bad, and couldn't figure out what it was," Jim said. "Then one day, Hill passed out from the pain. His woman said he'd been shot in a Texas gun fight. He wouldn't go to a doctor, and it got infected, and gangrene. She was begging us to help him. So I took him to Doc Carson at Fort Laramie. He amputated the arm, and that's all I'm gonna say about it." Big Jim didn't care to remember that morbid experience.

"So you don't know exactly what happened in Texas?" Arthur said.

"No. And we didn't have time to find out. I just left him and her there at the fort. Major Nelson was going to send him back to Texas. I guess maybe he didn't want to go back," Jim said.

"Tell me about your days as a wagon scout," Arthur said.

Big Jim took pride in his accomplishments as a wagon scout. He described in detail his trips to Oregon and California, and many of the adventures along the way.

"But the biggest wagon train was the 1843 group that come here," Jim said. "There was more going on with that wagon train than any other I've ever seen."

"I understand you met your wife on that trip," Arthur said.

"Sure did," Jim said. He told Arthur about his family, and the land they farmed.

George came back to give his report.

"Well, he's keeping to himself, mostly," George said. "He got something to eat, and a bottle of whiskey that he didn't pay for. Then he went over to Carolyn's Boarding House, and I guess he must've scared old James. He cleaned out the stable, and that's been it, so far."

"Thank you, George," Big Jim said. "Get you something to eat, and let's see what he does after dark."

Arthur went back to the Boarding House, and reviewed his notes.

74

It was ten thirty when Big Jim began his rounds. He walked out onto Main Street, and down past the bank. He felt a 'spooky feeling' that something wasn't right. The lantern and the moon gave good light, and he saw nothing wrong or out of place. He looked down 6th Street, and saw that everything was all right. He walked a little faster, and got past the Post Office and Drug Store. Jim shined his lantern around the corner of 5th Street and Main. The Livery Stable was just behind the meat market. Everything looked peaceful. He could hear the piano and the laughter from the bar at the billiard room. He walked on down to Main and 4th Street, crossed the street, and went back to his office. So far, so good.

At one o'clock, George saw something. He stood up, and saw a man coming out of the Livery Stable. The man walked in the shadows, and George followed silently on the other side of the street. The man went behind the bank building. George watched him push up a window, and put a rock there to hold it up. He looked around to see if anyone was watching. He carefully walked back to the Livery Stable. A horse snorted, and he calmed the animal, then closed the door.

George told Big Jim.

"He's gonna rob the bank," Jim said. "All right, George, stay with him. Me and Harry'll cover the bank from the front, you cover the back. Get in position around sun up."

George went back to his watch. Jim and Harry prepared extra guns and plenty of bullets.

James and Carolyn had their Boarding House open for breakfast by six o'clock. Helen and Susan helped cook and serve. Most of the breakfast guests were seated and eating when Ezra Hill walked in. Helen gasped. Susan stood frozen with suspense.

"Well, what are you looking at me for?" Ezra said. "I get hungry, too, you know. Can a body get something to eat around here?"

"Why sure, you can, Mr. Hill," Carolyn said.

"Mr. Hill," Ezra said. "I like that. Ain't nobody ever called me *Mister* before. You're a pretty sharp old woman. Say, you got any more of that ham and eggs? That sure does look good."

"I'll get you some," Carolyn said. She turned back to the kitchen.

"Just go on and do your job," Carolyn said. "It'll be all right. The Good Lord give His angels charge over us, and He'll protect us. Now, hand me that ham, please."

Carolyn brought him a plate of ham, eggs and biscuits. She poured the coffee, and a glass of water.

"Where's Libby?" she said.

"Huh?" Ezra said, between a mouthful of food.

"Libby Garrison. Where is she?" Carolyn said.

"Oh, I don't know," Ezra said. "The Army was sending us back to Texas. Got as far as Fort MacPhearson, and I got away from that stupid bunch. I don't know where she's at. Don't care, neither."

The tension was unbearable. No one knew how to act, or what to say. They certainly didn't want to upset him. He ate two plates full, and had three more cups of coffee.

"Well, that's a mighty fine breakfast, James," Ezra said. "Mighty fine, indeed."

He got up and left the table, with no offer to pay for the meal. No one wanted to challenge him.

George had climbed upon the roof of the bank building. He'd took out a piece of the roof, and lowered himself down onto the rafters above the vault and main offices. He fixed three shot guns at different angles, and tied the triggers to a string. He would pull the string, and fire all three guns at once. Over the tellers windows, he'd rigged two more rifles in the same manner. He could run between the two areas very quickly, and hopefully stop a robbery.

Big Jim took his position directly in front of the bank, on the other side of the street. Harry went to the north side of the shed, and George came down to the back of the bank, and stayed in the shadows. They knew the bank wouldn't open until nine. Mr. Wesley was always very prompt, and always went in through the front door.

They didn't have long to wait. As soon as Ezra finished breakfast, he went behind the bank, and pushed the window up. He crawled inside, and crept low to the floor. There was plenty of daylight now, and he could find the vault with ease.

George came out of the shadows, and signaled Big Jim by waving his arm. Then he scaled up a support pole, and onto the roof. George took the rope, and lowered himself down to the rafters. He watched Ezra pick the lock of the vault. It was harder than Ezra had expected, and he had to try two more times. Finally, he opened the vault. But the money was locked in yet another safe. George heard Ezra swearing, as he picked the lock.

Ezra laughed. "Oh, come to Papa," he said. Ezra grabbed a bank bag, and began stuffing it with the money. George heard coins jingling, as he watched thousands of dollars go into that bag.

Something hit the front door. It startled Ezra.

"Ezra Hill, come out now, and we won't shoot," Big Jim said.

"Is that you, Jim?" Ezra yelled. "If it is, why don't you come in here and get me?"

George retreated to the back where he could both pull the trigger strings, and get out on the roof as needed.

Arthur Kelly ran to Jim's side.

"Get down," Jim said. "Get behind that shed, stay out of the way, and don't you move until I tell you to."

Arthur was suddenly scared. He obey Jim's instructions without any objections.

The street was empty, and the town was still half asleep. There seemed to be a strange, unnatural quietness.

"All right, Jim, I'm coming out," Ezra said.

Jim and Harry cocked their guns. Jim motioned for Arthur to stay low, and to move back a little more. George picked up the string for the guns.

Ezra threw the sack of money over his shoulder, drew his pistol, and began firing at the bank's front door.

George pulled the two strings, and all five guns fired. George saw Ezra was hit in the heel of his left foot, and one bullet went through the sack of money on his back. No doubt that shot would have been fatal, if not for the money. Ezra fired again at the door. Jim and Harry returned fire. Ezra turned to go out the back window. George came out on the roof.

Ezra found the window had been closed, and realized he was trapped. He threw a chair through the window, and jumped out, rolling as he hit the ground. Blood poured from the wound in his heel, and now from a deep cut on his arm.

George couldn't bring himself to shoot a man in the back.

"Ezra," George said.

Hill looked up on the roof, and George fired. At nearly the same instant, Big Jim and Harry came around the corner, firing their weapons.

Arthur Kelly stood right beside Big Jim.

"I thought I told you to stay put," Jim said.

"You did," he said. "But this is just too important. I have to see what happens."

The life slowly drained from Ezra Hill. Jim bent over the lifeless form. He couldn't find a heartbeat.

"He's dead," Jim said.

A crowd had gathered, and stared at the dead man on the ground. Mr. Wesley came.

"Mr. Wesley, you take the banks money," Big Jim said. "Open up the bank, go in and count it, right now. Look around, and make sure nothing else is wrong in there."

The undertaker carriage arrived. Big Jim helped put Ezra in the carriage. He closed the door, and the carriage rolled on.

Arthur felt sick. He'd never witnessed death before. He ran to the nearest shed, leaned against the wall, and threw up until he could heave no more.

Big Jim went inside the bank, while George and Harry dispersed the crowd.

"Well, it's all here," Mr. Wesley said. "He would have cleaned us out. He put every last penny this bank has in that bag. How did you know he was going to do this?"

"Well, I've had a run-in with him before," Jim said.

They walked through the bank. The only other damage was the broken window and chair, and the shingles on the roof.

"I'm not worried about things like that, Jim," Mr. Wesley said. "I'm just glad it's over, and no one else got hurt."

"You boys look after the town today," Big Jim said to George and Harry. "I need to rest."

He went to Carolyn's Boarding House. Helen met him at the door.

"It's all over, honey," he said. He held her for a moment. "Is there a vacant room? I sure need some sleep."

George and Harry explained to John and Martha all that had transpired. In a few minutes, it was explained to Mr. Peterson and Councilman Dudley. Mr. Dudley offered to get Mr. Peterson a fresh, homemade pie.

"Don't you even think of bringing one of those things anywhere near me," Mr. Peterson said. "If you do, I'll have you and your wife thrown into jail for ever. Do you understand me?"

"Well, yes," Mr. Dudley said. "But I was just trying to be neighborly, and give you something good to eat."

"Well, they're not good to eat. Whatever she puts in them would probably kill a horse. Now, leave me alone," Mr. Peterson said.

"Arthur, you look sick," John said.

"I am sick, John," he said.

John emphasized. "I know just how you feel," he said.

The news spread quickly. It happened before most people came into town, and it was the first thing that confronted them

Martha went into the schoolhouse. Soon her students would arrive, and she needed to prepare today's lessons. But her mind went blank. She stared out the window, and tried to compose her scattered emotions. She heard the children laughing and playing out side. Gradually, her fears abated, and she began preparing her work.

7 GOLD

Martha noted that Becky and Jenny had made remarkable progress in their studies. Jenny's biggest problem was Charles. He still felt threatened. Their relationship grew more strained each day.

"Martha, what am I going to do?" Jenny said. "He won't even try to understand. It's got so bad that we can't even talk about anything no more."

"Are you sure you want to continue?" Martha said. "Maybe you should give him more time to think about this."

"He's too stubborn to ever change his mind," she said. "Besides, I figure if I don't do this now, I'll never get another chance. And I want to learn, Martha."

"Do you want me to talk to him?"

"No," Jenny said. "It won't do no good. And he'd just be mad at you, then."

"What about the rest of your family? Are they still supporting you and Becky?" Martha said.

"Yeah," she said. "In fact, Momma's done wrote to all our folks back home about us going to the Oregon Institute this fall. And I'm going, Martha. If Charles don't want me to go, that's just too bad, cause he ain't going to stop me."

The two hours Martha spent with Becky and Jenny were always productive. The girls had worked hard in all their subjects. They were still slow and awkward with Latin, but Martha was very pleased. Tonight she had some good news for her two students.

After their studies, Martha took out an envelope.

"Girls, let me share something with you," she said. She opened the envelope.

"I wrote to a friend in Paris," she said. "I told her about the two of you, and your desire for education. She agrees that you should have a chance to learn."

Martha took the check out of the envelope and put it on the table. "This check pays for all your expenses at the Oregon Institute," Martha said. "I know both of you will work hard, and graduate. My friend will ask about you every once in a while. I know you won't let her down."

The girls laughed and cried. They looked at the check, and could scarcely believe it.

"Oh, Martha," Becky said. "This is wonderful."

"Nobody's ever done anything like this for us," Jenny said. "Our family's always been poor. Momma said we was so poor we couldn't even pay attention. I don't rightly know what to say."

Before the girls went home, their younger brothers, Johnny and Oliver came by to visit.

"You girls still trying to talk in that Latin?" Johnny said.

"We sure are," Becky said. "And we're going to school this fall, too."

"Well, sure 'nuff," Oliver said. "Tell you what, girls, we got something a whole lot better than school."

"What?" Jenny said. To her, nothing could be more important than her chance to learn.

"Gold, silly," Johnny said. "We've been hearing about gold in that place called California. For the last two weeks, we been meeting a bunch of people talking about a big gold strike out there."

"And we thought we'd go get some," Oliver said.

"Boys, are you sure about this?" Martha said. She had only recently broken the addictive power of money, and couldn't stand the thought of seeing good young men ensnared in its trap.

"Yeah, we're sure," Johnny said. "There's an outfit coming through here in about a month, and they'll be hiring. And we aim to be going with them."

"You better tell Momma and Daddy," Becky said.

"Daddy may not want you to do this," Jenny said.

"Well, look at you," Oliver said. "Charles don't want you going to school, neither. But you're going to do it anyway. Ain't you?"

His remarks stung. Jenny started to argue the point. But Martha held up her hand, stopping it.

"I think Becky's right, boys," Martha said. "Talk it over with your family, first."

The girls finished their lessons, and returned to Carolyn's Boarding House.

When Patrick came to get Susan, he had a letter from home. She knew by the look on his face that it was bad news.

"That potato famine is awful," he said.

Susan didn't want to hear the rest of it, yet she knew she must.

"Father died in February," he said. "Ian and Coleen and the kids are coming here. They're bringing Mother with them. Ian said your Uncle Sean died, too."

Susan cried. "Sean was always my favorite uncle," she said. They cried all the way home, while trying to explain this to the children.

Malindy Miller had always insisted that her children eat Sunday dinner at home. This way, the family could all be together. Her family now included Bobby, Charles, Billy Joe, and Betty Sue. She adored her grandchildren, and Calvin spoiled them.

The dinner conversation was pleasant and light hearted.

"Guess this is as good a time as any to tell you all," Johnny said. "Me and Oliver's going to California, and work them gold mines."

"What?" Calvin said. "Son, that's mighty hard, dangerous work. And to top it off, you don't know nothing about mining. And I don't know nothing about it, either."

Malindy was shocked. She didn't want any of her children in a dangerous job, nor did she want them so far away from home.

"Honey, I don't think that's such a good idea," Malindy said.

"Well, you're letting Becky and Jenny go off to that school," Oliver said.

Charles nudged Jenny. "See there what that crazy notion of yours and Becky's started?" he said.

"Well, it ain't dangerous to go to school," she said.

"But it ain't going to do you no good, either," Charles said. "If you start talking in that there Latin, none of us can understand you."

Malindy gave them a very stern look. "Now, that's enough from you two," she said. "All you ever do is fight and argue anymore. If you just have to fight one another, then go some place else to do it."

"Yes, Ma'am," Charles said.

"I'm sorry, Momma," Jenny said. She could tell Charles was still mad. But she didn't want another argument with him.

"Daddy, if I'm supposed to be a man, and make a living on my own, then I have to go where I can make some money," Johnny said.

"And in California, we can make lots of money," Oliver said.

"Well, there's more to life than just making money," Calvin said. "You boys both got real good jobs here. Your family's all here. Why can't you work here?"

"Cause we can make more in California," Johnny said.

"I wish you'd think real hard about this," Malindy said.

"We have thought about it real hard," Oliver said. "And that's what we aim to do."

Malindy and Calvin saw that it was useless to argue with them. They let the subject drop.

"Mother, what do you think about me and Bobby starting up a cheese plant here in town?" Sarah said.

"Sounds good to me," she said.

"I'm getting ready to go back to the Nebraska Territory, and bring back another herd of cattle," Bobby said. "And when we get back with them, I'm going to start the cheese business."

Johnny started to offer his very biased opinion.

"Don't you dare say a word, young man," Sarah said. "I can still whip you awful hard, just like I did when you was little."

The entire family laughed, even Charles. Sarah had always picked fights with Johnny, and she usually won. Johnny would never challenge her.

The next day, Bobby and Sarah came into town. He needed to find a good place to house his new cheese venture. Sarah and the children visited with everyone at Carolyn's Boarding House.

"Well, hello, Bobby," he said.

Bobby turned and greeted Jerry Connelly. He remembered Jerry from the wagon train, but was very apprehensive about the man.

They visited for a few minutes, and Jerry asked what Bobby was doing now. Bobby told him about his plans for a cheese business, and bringing back a herd of cattle.

"Is there a road straight across the Territory from Fort Boise?" Jerry said.

"No, there ain't," Bobby said. "Big Jim said I'd have to cut my own trail."

"Have you ever done that?"

"No," Bobby said. He didn't like to admit it, but he had no idea how to do that.

"Well, I used to work with Sam Barlow," Jerry said. "Back in '45, I helped him cut that road over Mt. Hood. I'd be glad to help you, if you want me to."

"Thanks, Jerry," he said. "I need some help. Be right glad to have you along. We'll be ready in about a couple of weeks. Meet me at Carolyn's."

They shook hands, and Bobby was pleased. One problem was solved. Now he'd need four or five more men to help with the cattle drive.

Bobby had asked Johnny and Oliver to help with the cattle drive, but they'd refused. They were going to California, with gold in their sights, and nothing else interested them. He got two men from Oregon City, and found two more in the new Portland settlement. He leased a good building behind the General Merchandise Store. His preliminary work was finished, and all he needed was more cattle. Sarah and Malindy had agreed to help him get the cheese business up and going.

A wagon clattered up to the boarding house. The well dressed business man came inside.

"Pardon me, Ma'am," he said. "What would you charge a humble business man for one week's lodging here?"

"It's one dollar a week, sir," Carolyn said.

"If I don't stay all week, can you come down just a little?"

"If you don't stay the full week, come and talk to me," Carolyn said.

He paid, and she gave him a key.

"Your room is the last one down the hall, on the left," Carolyn said.

"Thank you kindly, Ma'am," he said. "Now, where can I leave my wagon and team?"

"You can leave the wagon around back, and the Livery Stable is just down the street."

He picked up his suit case, and went down the hall.

The next morning at breakfast, the new guest was up early. He came into the kitchen, and stood between Carolyn and Helen, and blocked Susan from reaching the stove.

"You know, you really need some new cooking pots," Mr. Brewster said. "I have just what you need out in the wagon. Let me show you some of my best merchandise."

"Wait a minute, Mr. Brewster," Carolyn said. "There's nothing wrong with what I'm using. Besides, I can't afford anything new right now."

"My good woman," he said. "You can't afford not to have these good solid, copper pots."

Carolyn was getting upset with him.

"No," she said firmly. "Mr. Brewster, I can't afford any of this."

He left the kitchen.

"Oh, I just can't stand these pushy drummers," Carolyn said.

"He's not staying here, is he?" Susan said.

"I'm afraid he is," Carolyn said.

Mr. Brewster came back in with two large copper pots.

"Here," he said. "I'll let you try these for a couple of days. You be the judge. See if they're not worth five dollars a piece."

"That's much too high," Carolyn said. "And I've already told you that I can't afford it. Now, take them back to your wagon, please."

"Good quality pots like these can make a real difference in how good the food tastes," he said.

"Sir, I can't buy any of your pots. I'm sure they're very good. But I can't afford them. Now, please excuse us. We have to fix your breakfast."

He just stood there in front of Carolyn. She was mad.

"Mr. Brewster," she said. "If you don't move out of my way, I'm going to use that carving knife on your scalp, just like the Indians do."

He moved.

"What's going on here?" Helen said.

Mr. Brewster had taken over the long breakfast table. He'd lined up bottles of tonic water, and tin boxes of salve. There were boxes of powders and pills, and herbs. He had so many things lined up that Helen couldn't put the food on the table.

Helen just turned, and took the food back to the kitchen.

"You ain't going to believe this," she said to Carolyn. "You've got to make him get that stuff off the table."

Carolyn lost her temper.

"Mr. Brewster," she yelled. "You get that stuff off my breakfast table, right now. If you don't, sir, I will go get the Sheriff."

"Now, now," he said. "These are all my miracle cures. Why these medicines have cured all kinds of diseases. I believe people want to stay healthy. These things will help you feel better, and live longer."

"Well, you ain't going to live very long if you don't get them off my table," she said.

The guests were coming in for breakfast. Some were looking at Mr. Brewster's products. James brought in more wood for the kitchen stove, and came to see what was going on.

"How much is this?" Mrs. Palmer asked.

"That's five dollars for a mighty good salve," Brewster said.

Mrs. Palmer paid him. Mr. Palmer paid ten dollars for a bottle of tonic.

"That tonic is the finest medicine in the world," Brewster said. "Better get two bottles, before I run out. A body never knows when they'll get sick, and really need this good tonic. It cures everything."

He sold six bottles of tonic, three boxes of salve, and numerous boxes of powders and pills.

"Ok, Mr. Brewster," James said. "Clear this table so these folks can eat breakfast. If you don't, we'll have to go get the Sheriff."

Several people grabbed bottles and boxes, then stuffed the appropriate amount of money in his hand. They had bought almost all of what he had. He set the four remaining boxes of herbs beside his chair.

Breakfast was served.

Mr. Brewster took his wagon down Main Street, and stopped at the corner of 6th and Main. There he began selling copper pots and pans, and his collection of 'medicines' and cures.

By noon, Big Jim had received dozens of complaints regarding the potency of Brewster's medical concoctions, the quality of his pots and pans, and the prices of all these items. He decided to investigate.

There was still a crowd of people around Brewster's wagon. Big Jim spotted Dr. Morgan coming toward the wagon. Jim waved to him. Dr. Morgan walked over to Jim.

"What in the Sam Hill's going on here, Jim?" Dr. Morgan said.

"Snake Oil salesman," Jim said. "If I was a betting man, I'd lay odds it's whiskey in them bottles. What do you say we take a closer look? Go buy a bottle of his 'world famous tonic'."

Dr. Morgan bought a bottle of tonic, a box of pills, and a box of salve. Big Jim opened the bottle, and took a drink. He spit it out, and gaged.

"Rot-gut," Jim said. "And I think it's bad rot-gut, too. What's the pills, Doc.?"

Dr. Morgan crushed a pill in his hand, and tasted a tiny portion.

"Sugar pills," he said. He smelled the salve, and tasted a little of it. "Some kind of grease mixed with flour."

Big Jim pushed his way through the crowd, and stood before Mr. Brewster.

"All right, Brewster," he said. "I've had nothing but complaints against you all morning long. Now, I'm shutting you down, right now."

The crowd jeered.

"He's selling you rot-gut," Jim said. "Did any of you drink his so-called tonic?"

No one had drank it, no one had tasted the pills and powders.

Big Jim continued. "He's selling rot-gut whiskey in them tonic bottles. Doc. Morgan says the pills are sugar pills, and that salve is grease and flour."

"Hey, just a minute, here," Brewster said. "What do you think you're doing? I make my living selling these fine products. This tonic has completely cured lots of folks, and so have these good pills. You can't just shut me down."

"Yes, I can shut you down," Big Jim said. "You're cheating these good folks, and I don't aim to let you do it any more. Now, get that stuff put back in your wagon, and get out of this town."

"But, but, you can't do this."

Big Jim drew his gun. "Yes, I can do this," he said. "Now, before you go, you're going to give refunds to anybody that wants a refund. I'll get one of my deputies to ride you out of town."

"I want a refund," shouted one man. "I sure don't want no rot-gut."

Others joined in asking for refund, yet some were satisfied with their purchase. In a few minutes, all transactions were finished. George arrived, and escorted Mr. Brewster out of town.

8 THE POWDER MONKEY

Martha needed to get Becky and Jenny back to the Oregon Institute to pay their tuition. She'd let the deadline slip up on her, and now there were only two days left.

"Hurry, girls," Martha said. They climbed into the wagon, and she kissed her children good-bye at the boarding house. Becky and Jenny were excited, and laughter filled the morning.

They arrived on campus late in the afternoon. Martha was a little worried that no one would be in the office. She didn't dare let the girls see her apprehension, so she boldly knock on the door.

"Enter," the voice said.

"I'm Mr. Phillips," he said. "May I help you?"

Martha nudged Becky, and she stepped up to his desk.

"Yes, sir," she said. The nervousness was evident. Her voice quivered a little, and she glanced back at Martha.

Martha's gestures indicated for Becky to proceed.

"I'm Becky, uh, Rebecca Miller," she said. "I"m here to pay my tuition."

"All right," he said. "I usually teach science. But today, I'm helping out in the office." He frantically looked for the Registration Book, and the receipt book. Finally he found the Registration Book.

"Here we are," he said. "And you're Rebecca Miller. Yes, here it is. Did you just want to pay for part of the first year?"

Becky looked helpless.

"No, sir," Martha said. "These girls are paying the complete four year tuition."

"You can't be serious."

"I most certainly am serious," Martha said. Martha got out the information they'd been given on their first visit to the Oregon Institute. She handed Mr. Phillips the financial worksheet, and he studied it. He added the numbers, and his answers agreed with the worksheet.

"Well, young lady, let me find the receipt book," he said. He dug through three stacks of papers and books until he found it.

Becky had opened her purse, and had the money in her hand. She put the stacks of cash on his desk. Mr. Phillips stared in amazement. He began counting the money.

"Can, can I have a receipt, please," Becky said.

He wrote the receipt without comment, and gave it to Becky.

"Thank you, sir," she said. She put it in her purse, and walked back to Martha.

Jenny stepped up. Her confidence had grown stronger as she watched her sister.

"And what is your name, young lady?"

"I'm Virginia Miller, and I'm paying all of my tuition, too," she said.

Martha gave him the financial worksheet for Jenny. He saw that everything was in order. He counted the money she gave him, and wrote out the receipt.

"Now, fall classes start promptly on September 10th," he said. "Are either of you going to live on campus? If so, you'll need to register, and get your dorm room on August 20th. I trust that you'll both be here promptly."

"Oh, yes, sir," Becky said.

The ride home was happy and exciting for them. Martha was delighted.

"Martha, we couldn't have done this without you," Jenny said.

"Oh, yes, you could have," Martha said. "You're both very determined, and you want to learn. I'm very proud of you two."

Becky and Jenny sat down to supper with Billy Joe and Charles.

"Say, Becky, I've been thinking," Billy Joe said. "I think I figured out a way you can go to school, and have a place to live, too."

"Oh?" she said.

"Yeah," he said. "Big Jim told me about the fruit farms they've got up there around that school. He said there's apple and peach orchards, and hazelnuts, and gooseberries, too. I could get me a job at one of them places, and you could go to school. Course, now, you'd have to marry me."

Becky gasped. "Marry you? Of course I will!" She turned over the gravy bowl as she jumped up and ran around the table to him. There was gravy all over her dress, and all over the floor. But she didn't care.

Charles never said a word. He just kept eating. Occasionally, he'd look at Jenny, but he couldn't look in her eyes. The fractured relationship was just about at it's end. Charles finished his meal, excused himself, and walked outside.

A few moments later, Billy Joe came out. They leaned against the old pine tree in the yard.

"What about it, Charles?" Billy Joe said. "Me and you can work in them orchards, and make a living while the girls go to school. Me and you'll have to make the living anyway, cause there ain't much around here for a woman to work at, no way."

"Then why does she want to do this?" he said. "All that money she wasted today on that tuition, whatever that is. We could've took that and bought us some land, and built a house, maybe got some cattle, or something. What's she doing this for?"

Billy Joe thought for a moment.

"When I was just a little bitty tyke, I wanted me a Bowie knife like my Daddy had," he said. "Daddy told me I'd have to save up my money, and buy one. So, I worked and worked for almost a year, and I finally got enough to buy that knife. That thing sure felt good in my pocket. But you know, I never did use that knife for a dog-gone thing. Never whittled anything, never skinned a possum or scaled a fish, or nothing with it."

"Then what'd you buy it for?" Charles said.

"Cause I wanted it," he said. "This is just something she wants real bad, like my Bowie knife. She may not ever use it, but it'll sure feel good in her pocket."

"It's always what *she* wants," Charles said. "When do I ever get what I want?"

"Well, what do you want?"

"I want a home and a family," he said. "I'm just a country boy, and I don't want no fancy, high society woman for a wife."

"Now, wait a second, Charles," Billy Joe said. "Jenny's not like that. And this ain't going to change her. When she's through school, she'll still be the same sweet woman she is right now. I don't want to see you loose the best thing that ever happened to you. Think about it, my friend. Now, let's get back in there, or they'll come out here after us."

They went back inside. Charles sat down beside Jenny. He took her hand, and gently kissed her cheek. She smiled at him, and the tension between them eased a little.

Bobby and his group left for the cattle drive. Jerry Connelly would take his group of workers as far as Fort Boise. Then they would clear a road out of the wilderness. When Bobby arrived later in the fall, his cattle would have an easy passage home.

Sunday dinner at Calvin and Malindy's was especially lively today

Johnny and Oliver couldn't wait to tell their family. Soon, they'd be leaving for California. Before long, they'd be rich beyond their wildest dreams.

"Son, what kind of job did you sign up for?" Calvin asked.

"I'm a powder monkey, Daddy," Johnny said.

"Oh, Lord, help us, now," Calvin said. "Boy, don't you know what that is?"

"Sure, Daddy," he said. "I'm in charge of the dynamite, and the blasting."

"Do they aim to show you how to do that?"

"Well, yeah, I guess so," Johnny said. "Besides, how hard can it be? You just light the fuse, and run fast as you can."

"What about you, Oliver? What'd they talk you into?" Calvin said.

"I'm helping Johnny," he said. "I carry the dynamite, gun powder, and the matches. He puts the stuff together, and crams it down in the mine shaft. Then we run like scared jack rabbits."

Malindy felt faint. "You boys is fixing to get in some real bad trouble, maybe even get hurt," she said. "I don't want you to go. Something just don't feel right."

"Oh, Momma," Johnny said. "Quit your worrying. We'll be all right. Ain't nothing going to happen to us."

"When are you going?" she said.

"Next Monday morning," Oliver said.

"Will you promise me to write to us every day?" Malindy said.

"Sure," Johnny said. "We'll write. Besides, I want to know if Bobby can get them cattle home."

Becky and Billy Joe began planning their wedding. Jenny and Charles were still at the same impasse. But at least, they were talking now. Malindy

99

wanted her girls to be happy. She began giving them bits of motherly advise.

"Honey, just be patient with Charles," she said. "He's a good man, and he'll work his way through this. Just you wait and see. But don't you give an inch. You dig them heels in, and stand your ground. I know this means so much to you. And I don't think he'd want you to just give up on it, or anything else you want real bad. I believe he'd really want his wife to hang on till she got what she wanted. Just try it, and see."

"Thanks, Momma," Jenny said. "I love you."

"And another thing both of you better remember," she said. "Now, it's always been a man's world, and it always will be. But us girls is actually the ones that has to do everything. I told this to Sarah, when her and Bobby married, and I'm telling you girls, now. Us girls have got to kind of caper around what men think, and get the job done ourselves, cause they'll mess around, and won't do it a lot of times. So, to get around it, a woman's got to always act like a lady, think like a man, and work just like a dog. Reckon you both can do that?"

They laughed.

"Sure we can, Momma," Becky said. "We've been doing it all our lives."

Johnny and Oliver were waiting for Mr. Williams in front of the Post Office. Oliver was excited and fidgety, but Johnny was subdued. He couldn't stand to see his Mother cry. He realized she really was concerned for them, and that bothered him. But it was too late to back out, now.

"Good morning, gentlemen," Williams said. "I see you're ready. We'll leave in about half an hour."

"We're ready, sir," Johnny said.

Williams went to the bank, and Big Jim ambled by.

"You boys know what you're getting into?" Jim said.

"Well, we ain't never done nothing like this before," Johnny said. "But I reckon we can learn how."

"Now, you be careful with that dynamite," Jim said. "Accidents can happen before you know what's going on."

"Yes, sir," Oliver said. "We'll be careful."

When Mr. Williams returned, they mounted their horses, and left for California.

9 CATTLE KING

Bobby Parker wanted the biggest and best cattle ranch in the Oregon Territory. If he could bring home another herd of one hundred cattle, he'd be very pleased. Big Jim had recommended Newt Moore, and Jeremiah Brown. Bobby didn't know them personally, but Jim said they were good men. The Sheriff in Portland had recommended Mack Thompson, and Bill White. Now Bobby would have to trust these men.

He still felt uneasy about Jerry Connelly. But Jerry soon quieted his fears.

"Bobby, how well do you know Thompson and White?" Jerry said.

"I don't know them," he said. "The Sheriff in Portland said they was good men. Why? Something wrong?"

"Well, I don't rightly know," he said. "Watch how they stay together, and don't have much to do with the other men. I don't like that."

"Yeah, I seen that," Bobby said. "We're just two days out of Oregon City, and they act like they don't want to be friendly."

"Bobby, I know you remember what happened on the wagon train," Jerry said.

Bobby nodded.

"I'm not the same man," Jerry said. "The good Lord's forgive me of my sins, and I'm preaching His Word whenever and where ever I can. I'll help you all I can, Bobby. I sure don't want to see anything go wrong for you."

Bobby thanked him. He kept his eye on White and Thompson from then on.

Jerry's group stopped at Fort Boisie. From the fort, they'd begin to cut a dug-way road back to Oregon City. It would be just wide enough for the wagons and animals, and would take most of the summer and fall to build.

Bobby's group went on to the Ogallala village, in the Nebraska Territory. There, the Oregon Trail converged with the Chislm and Goodnight cattle trails from Texas. Ranchers from the new territories would come to purchase livestock, and drive them back to the various western ranges. Bobby knew the Ogallala area was a wild, rough cow-town. He knew his men would likely end up in numerous bar room brawls, and probably even in jail. He was prepared for that, but hoped it wouldn't happen.

They reached their destination sooner than expected. They'd had good travel weather, and encountered no problems along the trail. They camped about a mile outside of town. They fixed a rabbit stew for supper.

"All right men," Bobby said. "Have any of you ever been here before to buy cattle?"

None of them had.

"Now, when we ride into town tomorrow, you'll find a lot of saloons, bar girls, poker games and whiskey," Bobby said. "I'm not paying you to get drunk, and raise a ruckus. If you end up in jail, we'll just leave you there. You get in trouble, and you can get out of it the best way you can. I don't want to see nobody get hurt, so be careful."

"I'm not some little boy," Thompson said. "And you sure ain't my mammy. You ain't nothing but a kid yourself. And I'm not taking orders from a boy."

"Then you ain't going to be paid by this boy, either," Bobby said.

"Ah, leave the kid alone," Moore said. "He got us here safe and sound. Besides, I know he runs that cattle ranch out of Oregon City. I think the boy knows what he's doing."

"Why don't you just stay out of this," Thompson said.

"What you do on your own time is your business," Bobby said. "But I'm not going to bail you out of jail, and I'm not going to pay you while you're drunk. I'm going to buy the cattle, bring them back here to camp, and start for home the next morning. If you're not sober enough to ride, you'll stay here. All right, let's get some sleep. We'll get started right after breakfast."

Booby spent a restless night. He wanted these cattle, and his plans were so big. He was anxious, and nervous.

They rode into town. It was late July, and the morning was already hot and dusty. There was a saloon everywhere he looked, and they all had a loud piano. Two men were fighting in an alley. No one paid any attention to the fight. They heard a gunshot. Bobby turned to look down the alley. Both men lay on the ground, and he couldn't tell which man had been shot.

104

The stock yard was on the other side of town, and Bobby's eye was on that. He got careless, and never knew when Thompson and White stopped at a saloon.

"Well, hello honey," the woman said. "Ain't you a bit young? I've got a son older than you."

"I'm just here to buy cattle," Bobby said.

"Yeah. That's what they all say," she said.

Brown and Moore stepped between her and Bobby, and Brown nudged him on to the buyers section.

"Keep going, Bobby," he said. "The more you talk to them, the worse it gets."

Bobby found a man selling cattle one hundred at a time. He asked what kind they were, and wanted to see them. Brown and Moore agreed to go with him.

Mr. Shaw took them to a herd of cattle just outside of town.

"These are my cattle. They're branded with the Rocking S," he said.

They walked out to the herd, and Bobby looked them over carefully. He pointed out four animals that he didn't like. Mr. Shaw cut them out of the herd. They counted out one hundred animals, at one dollar each. Bobby, Moore and Brown started back to camp with them.

"We'd better find White and Thompson," Brown said.

They spotted their horses, and Brown started in to get them.

"We ought to get this herd back to camp, first," Moore said. "Worry about them two later."

"He's right," Bobby said. "I'll come back and get them after a while."

105

They got the cattle back to camp, and settled them down. While Brown did the cooking, Bobby and Moore went back to town. Bobby gave Moore enough money to buy a wagon and food staples, and enough oats to get them to Fort Laramie. He'd planned to re-supply again at Laramie.

Bobby walked into the saloon. White was passed out at a back table. Thompson was in the middle of a poker game.

"Ready to go, Thompson?" Bobby said.

"Beat it, kid," he said, as he bit down on his cigar.

"Remember what I told you? If you get in trouble, I don't know you," Bobby said.

"Yeah, yeah," Thompson said

"All right," Bobby said. "If that's the way you want it. I'll see you around, sometime."

Bobby returned to camp just ahead of Moore and the new wagon. He told them about Thompson and White.

"I don't like those two," Bobby said. "They've acted plumb strange ever since we left home."

"Yeah," Moore said. "Better watch them. They might try something."

Bobby figured he'd get home with this herd about mid-November, if the weather stayed good. He'd feed them through this winter, and maybe they'd gain back the weight they'd loose on this cattle drive. Then next spring, he could count on good milk production. His cheese plant would be up and running this winter, and he felt good about his future.

Brown had the coffee made before sun up. He'd just panned the bacon when he looked up and saw White and Thompson galloping into camp.

They rode past the camp, got out their ropes, and began cutting out cattle from the herd.

"Hey," Bobby yelled. "What do you think you're doing?"

Moore and Brown ran after them, but it was too late. White and Thompson had rustled fifteen good cows, and were driving them away.

Bobby aimed his rifle.

"Easy, son," Brown said, as he pushed the rifle barrel down. "Them two ain't worth it. Let 'em go."

Bobby was angry and frustrated, but he knew Brown was right.

Moore went to town to report the theft.

"Well, what of it?" the Sheriff said.

"Then you ain't going to do nothing about it?"

"Nope."

Brown was aghast. "Well, why not?"

"Look, Mister," the Sheriff said. "I got one deputy, and no jail to speak of. What would I do with them if I caught them? Take the cows you got left, and go home."

Moore returned to camp, and told Bobby the Sheriff's comments.

Bobby was fighting mad. Moore and Brown had to restrain him. They wrestled him to the ground.

"I know you're mad," Brown said. "I'm mad, too. But there ain't nothing we can do about it. Now, come on, Bobby. Settle down. The three of us got to get these cattle home."

Bobby vented his anger on a rock by kicking it out of his way. He kicked over the horse's water bucket, and kicked over the coffee pot.

"Hey," Moore said. "You just spilled all my coffee."

"Let him alone," Brown said. "Let him get it out of his system, and get it over with."

Bobby walked back to the campfire.

"All right," he said. "Let's get going."

Bobby's cattle drive made good progress. A few days later, they pulled into Fort Laramie for supplies. Major Nelson remembered Bobby.

"Good to see you, Bobby," Major Nelson said. "Tell me about everyone on the wagon train, especially Big Jim and Helen."

Bobby informed him. "Remember Ezra Hill?" Bobby said.

"Of course I do," Major Nelson said. "I'll never forget him."

"Well, he showed up in Oregon City a few days before we left," Bobby said. He recounted the attempted bank robbery and shoot-out.

"Ezra's dead as a door-nail," Bobby said.

"What happened to Libby?" Major Nelson said. "Was she with him?"

"No. He told Mrs. Green that he escaped at Fort MacPhearson. Said he didn't know where she was, and didn't care," Bobby said.

"Nobody had any quarrel with her," Nelson said. "She'd be free to do whatever she wants."

"Yeah," Bobby said. "We all felt sorry for her. She seemed like a decent woman."

Bobby thought for a moment.

"Say, maybe you can help me," he said.

"I'd be glad to."

Bobby explained about the stolen cattle.

He got out the bill of sale. "They're all branded with Mr. Shaw's Rocking S brand." Bobby drew a crude picture of the brand.

"Thank you," Major Nelson said. "Can you describe White and Thompson to me? I can't do much about the cattle. But if these characters show up in my territory, I'll arrest them."

Bobby described them, and then it was time to leave.

"Good luck, Bobby," Nelson said. "Anytime you're back this way, stop by for a visit. You're always welcome here. Now, be sure you tell Big Jim and Helen hello for me."

"I will," Bobby said. "Thanks again, sir." They shook hands, and Bobby's cattle drive rolled out of Fort Laramie.

The next few weeks brought them near the Green River. Until now, Bobby had kept them away from bad water, but three cows were sick.

"Let's put an end to their suffering," Brown said.

"I don't think I can shoot them," Bobby said.

"Yes, you can. They'll die in a day or two, anyway. Take care of it now, and we won't suffer along with them," Brown said.

Bobby fired three shots. He walked away and cried.

"Come on, Bobby," Brown said. "Don't look back. Let's just go on home. Fort Bridger ain't too far off, now."

Bobby's wagon pulled into Fort Bridger, and he bought supplies. He was very homesick, and he went to the Bridger Trading Post to find gifts for Sarah and the kids.

On his way out the door, he bumped into another man.

"Well, for goodness sakes," Bobby said. "Paul Smith. Is that you, Paul?"

"Bobby, I sure didn't expect to see you again," Paul said. "What are you doing here?"

Bobby explained.

"Where's Jake?" Bobby said.

"Jake's here, somewhere," Paul said. "He's probably asleep somewhere, though. He ain't been himself lately."

"What do you mean?" Bobby said.

"Well, it's a long story. His mind ain't just right, nowadays," Paul said "He's been wanting to go to Oregon City, and see Jim. I didn't want him wandering around out here by himself, so I came along."

Bobby had an idea.

"Well, I'm taking this herd of cattle back home to Oregon City. Reckon you and Jake can help me get them there?" Bobby said.

"Why, sure, we can," Paul said. "This'll really make him feel better, Bobby. I tell you, he's been having a real hard time."

They found Jake asleep in the stable. Paul finally got him awake.

"Jake, you remember Big Jim's wagon train, don't you?" Paul said.

"Yeah. Yeah, I remember the biggest wagon train to leave Independence," Jake said.

"Remember that blond headed boy with all them cattle?" Paul said.

"I sure do. Is that you, Bobby?"

Bobby shook Jake's hand. He noted a confused, far away look in Jake's eyes.

"Jake, I'd sure like for you and Paul to help me get these cattle home to Oregon City," Bobby said.

"Why sure," Jake said. "We can do it. When you leaving?"

"We're leaving this morning," Bobby said. "Just as soon as I get back to camp with our supplies. You two get your things together, and follow me out to camp."

There wasn't many 'things' to get together. All that Paul and Jake had were their clothes, saddles and horses. They were ready in a few minutes.

Bobby marveled at his good fortune in finding Paul and Jake. He proudly introduced them to Moore and Brown.

"Good looking herd, Bobby," Jake said.

"Yeah, they're a good bunch," he said. Bobby "Rustlers got fifteen of them. And to think it was men I hired to ride with me."

"Well, you don't have to worry 'bout us, none," Jake said.

"You're Jake Carter, the wagon scout, ain't you?" Moore said.

"Yeah. Me and Big Jim's took wagons all over the place out here. Me and him took one group to California a few years ago. And me and Paul took a group from Jim's '43 wagon train on to California," Jake said. He was pleased that people remembered his work.

"Big Jim's mentioned you several times," Moore said.

"What's Jim doing now?" Jake said.

As they broke camp, they told Jake and Paul all the news from Oregon City. Bobby was thankful to have four men he knew he could trust. He knew the rest of the journey home would be easier, now.

10 A FEISTY LITTLE WOMAN

Arthur Kelly had spent the past several weeks around the Portland settlement. He'd learned the history of the Pacific northwest from Dr. John McLoughlin, and spent some time at Fort VanCouver. After the Barlow Road was opened over Mt. Hood, the fort wasn't as busy as it used to be. Arthur had pressed Dr. McLoughlin about when England might give up her colonial claims of these western territories. It made McLoughlin mad, but provided good fuel for the newspapers back home.

Arthur had told Dr. McLoughlin of his meetings with Martha, sketching her classroom, her children, and many other things. He informed the doctor that in the Boston social circles, Martha had quite a reputation. Dr. McLoughlin's reply was that Martha was indeed '*a feisty little woman.*' Arthur knew that phrase would make a good headline. He'd just finished a thumb-nail sketch of Martha. She'd provided some excellent insight into every subject he brought up.

He was especially intrigued by her views of women's suffrage. Martha's opinions were not the prevailing thought of the day. She believed that women should be educated equally with men. That's why she was helping Becky and Jenny with their schooling. She believed women should be paid as much as men, especially if they did the same job. Martha knew women could be doctors, lawyers, politicians and theologians, engineers and scientists.

Every time he raised an objection, she countered with good, solid evidence. He couldn't argue against that evidence. He couldn't find anything wrong in her public or private life. He had to admit to himself that this feisty little woman was genuine. She was the same temperament at work, at home, or at church. At first, this irritated him. He'd never met anyone he couldn't shake their confidence, get them rattled and upset. In fact, Martha was the one who could rattle him. Her ability to take any statement he made, turn it around, and use it against him was just uncanny. Once, he'd thought about asking John his secret to getting along with her. But he realized he didn't dare risk it. Gradually, Arthur began to admire and respect her.

"Martha, would you like to attend a lecture on women's suffrage with me?" Arthur said. He knew he'd just opened the door for her. On one hand, he knew she would chew him up, and spit him out. But, on the other hand, it would be the most challenging conversation he'd ever get on this subject.

"I'd love to," Martha said. "Is it Mrs. Young that I've been reading so much about?"

"Yes, it is," Arthur said. "She'll be over at Salem Saturday afternoon, at the Institute. I thought you'd enjoy that."

"Yes, I will," she said. "We'll see you then."

Martha wanted Jenny and Becky to attend the lecture.

"You can go with us," Martha said. She explained a little about women's suffrage to them.

"We don't know anything about this," Becky said.

"Well, this is one way to learn new things," Martha said. "Just listen to this lady. Later, we'll discuss what you think about it."

"What if we don't agree with her?" Jenny said.

"It's all right to disagree with her," Martha said. "And, it's all right to agree with what she says. But I want both of you to think about her ideas, and make up your own minds. It's very important to think for yourself."

Martha, John and the girls arrived at the lecture. Jenny and Becky were excited. They had looked forward to this all week. They were well dressed, and looked lovely. Martha was delighted.

Martha and John waved to Arthur. He made his way through the crowd, and joined them. Martha made the proper introductions.

Arthur started to ask Becky out to dinner. Martha caught that look in his eye. She shook her head 'no', and he looked puzzled.

Martha stepped closer to him, and pretended to brush something off his jacket. "They're both engaged," she whispered.

He looked disappointed, but recovered immediately. Arthur and John began talking about the possibility of Oregon statehood.

Martha took Becky and Jenny into the ladies room.

"All right, girls," she said. "Now listen to me. Arthur Kelly is a newspaper reporter from Boston."

"Oh, my goodness," Becky said. "He's the one you've been talking about. Ain't he?"

"That's right," Martha said. "Everything you say to him just might end up in the newspapers in Boston. When you speak, be sure you say exactly what you mean. Now, try to relax, and just be yourselves."

They exchanged glances.

"But what'll we talk about?" Jenny said.

"Be honest, and answer his questions. As your mother would say, 'don't put on airs'. You'll do just fine," Martha said.

Martha sat between Arthur and John. Jenny was on Arthur's left, and Becky sat beside John.

Arthur was very curious about their opinions, and found it hard to hold back his reporters instincts.

"Jenny, what do you think about Mrs. Young's ideas?" he said.

"Well, I don't rightly know," she said. "I ain't heard her speak yet."

Good girl, Jenny Martha thought. *That was the perfect answer. Just keep it up all night.*

Mrs. Young's ideas were radical, even for Martha. In fact, she was offended by several things. She could tell John was getting embarrassed. But, it seldom took much to embarrass him. She thought Arthur seemed amused.

Martha was almost afraid to look at Jenny and Becky. What would Malindy think of her if she knew the contents of this lecture? Would the girls even tell her?

115

After the lecture, Arthur stayed to interview Mrs. Young. Martha was glad, for she wanted to gage her students opinions for herself.

"Well, girls," Martha said. "What do you think?"

"Well, I think she's crazier than a bed bug," Becky said. "But still, I agree with her about some of it. Lots of things need to change, Martha. But Lordy Mercy, I wouldn't stand up there and talk about it like that."

"Now, wait, Becky," Jenny said. "I like her. It takes a lot of nerve to do what she's doing, and I like that. Sometimes what she said embarrassed me. But she told the truth. She said what we all think sometimes. I don't like the way she said it, but I agree with her."

"I'm glad you listened," Martha said. "Think about these things, and see what you can learn from this experience. We'll talk more about it this coming week."

They said good night to Becky and Jenny, but they were both silent the rest of the way home.

"John, did I do wrong by getting two unsophisticated country girls in over their heads?" Martha said, as they prepared for bed. "I was in over my head, to say nothing of them."

"No, dear," John said. "You didn't do anything wrong. In the first place, you had no way to know exactly what she'd say, and you couldn't control how she said it. They're grown women, and they handled it very well. Now, don't worry about it."

Martha's mind could envision the headlines in the Boston paper. Her sleep was filled with nightmarish scenes of her father scolding her for attending such a lecture. Then Malindy reprimanded her in another nightmare. Carolyn chided her relentlessly for being a bad influence to all the little girls in Oregon City.

Martha woke up. *I didn't bring that woman here, and I didn't write her notes* she thought. *I may agree with a lot of what she said, but I don't have to like the way she did it.*

Martha decided to tell Malindy about the lecture.

"Why, honey, it's all right," Malindy said. "My kids all knows that the world ain't no bed of roses. They all know that not everybody's going to be good, or nice to them. What all did they say about it?"

Martha gave her the general idea of what Jenny and Becky had expressed.

"Sounds like they took it in stride," Malindy said. "All my kids have got a mind of their own. That's the way we taught them to be. They'll be all right. And just maybe, they'll learn a thing or two. Now, you quit your worrying about this, you hear me?"

"Yes, Ma'am."

11 CAN'T YOU HEAR 'EM CALLIN'

Bobby was anxious to get home. He was tired. Lately, he'd wondered if being a cattle king was worth all these hardships. Now there was the added burden of knowing something was wrong with Jake. He decided that Dr. Morgan needed to examine Jake, if Jake would agree.

Oregon City was just two miles ahead. Moore and Brown rode up beside Bobby.

"Well, boss," Moore said. "You showed me a thing or two, Bobby. I've watched you every day for nearly five months, now. You're a mighty good man, and I'm proud to work for you."

Bobby shook his hand.

"Would you like to be my foreman?" Bobby said. "How 'bout it, Brown? I need you, too. I want men I can trust. You've both proved yourselves to me."

They accepted Bobby's offer with pleasure.

Bobby looked back at Paul and Jake.

"I'm going to get them two settled in Carolyn's Boarding House," he said. "Then I'm going to drag Jake to Dr. Morgan's house. There's something wrong with him, and I can't hardly stand it. You two help me get these cattle in my pasture, and we'll settle up. Then go on home. I'll pay Connelly for his work."

James saw Bobby ride up with two men. He greeted Bobby, and shook their hands.

"You don't remember me, do you?" Paul said. "I'm Paul Smith."

"It's sure good to see you, Paul," he said. "Jake? Is that you, Jake?" James was surprised to see them.

"Yeah, it's me, James," Jake said. "How you doing?"

They talked for a moment, and James took them inside. Bobby waited until they went to their room.

"James, I think Jake's sick, or something," he said. "Sometimes he acts all right, and other times, he don't. I'll see if I can get him to Dr. Morgan."

Carolyn, Helen and Susan fixed them a special meal for supper. Big Jim brought the children with him. Jake gave the kids a pony ride on his shoulders, and Paul played games with them. The evening was filled with pleasure, as old friends visited and laughed.

Bobby jumped off his horse before she even stopped. He ran to the door. The dog barked, and wagged his tail. Bobby stopped long enough for the dog to bounce in his arms, and lick his face. Then he saw her.

"Bobby," Sarah said. "Oh, please don't ever be gone this long again."

They both cried.

"Don't worry," Bobby said. "I won't ever be gone from home that long no more."

Jake's screams woke everyone up. Paul was at his side immediately.

"Jake, Jake," Paul said. He slapped Jake's face hard. "Jake," he yelled. "Wake up, Jake. It's all right, now. You're safe, now. We're all safe."

Jake sat up in the bed, and began to cry. He sobbed so hard that it shook the bed, and he broke out in a cold sweat. Paul used his bandana to mop the sweat from Jake's face.

The guests had crowded in the hallway, just outside Paul and Jake's room. James went in to check on Jake. Carolyn had the baby, and Jane began to cry. Two of the other ladies helped Carolyn feed her and change her.

"Anything we can do, Paul?" James said.

"I…I don't know, James," Paul said. "I never know just what to do when he gets like this. Out on the trail, they'd give him whiskey to calm him down."

"Did that help?" James said.

"Sometimes," he said. "If we can ever calm him down, he'll go back to sleep, and be all right."

James went out in the hallway.

"Anybody got some whiskey?" he said.

Jake began crying again.

"Oh, God, Paul," he cried. "Can't you hear 'em callin'? Can't you hear 'em beggin' for something to eat? My God, Paul, look at them poor people. What are we going to do, Paul?"

"Jake, calm down," Paul said. "It's all right, now."

Someone handed Paul a flask of whiskey.

"Here," Paul said. "Drink this."

Jake swallowed half the whiskey. "Thank you, my friend," he said. He drank the rest of it, and sank into inebriation. They laid him back on the bed, and Jake passed out.

Paul and James closed the door, and went into the kitchen.

"All right, folks," James said. "Let's go back to bed."

Carolyn put her arm around Paul.

"Paul, what in the world is wrong with him?" she said.

"I think he's just plumb lost his mind," Paul said.

"How did this happen?"

James sat down beside them.

Paul sighed. He didn't like to remember it, either. But James and Carolyn and all their friends deserved an explanation.

"Well, last year, me and Jake was taking a group to California," Paul said. "Some of the group got sick, and pulled off the road. They was several days behind the main group. I took the main group on over the mountains, and down to the Truckee Valley. Jake went back to help the rest of them catch us with us. Jake and them got caught in an early snow storm high up in the mountains. Jake was there, and he seen it all."

Paul stopped, and choked back the tears. "James, all them people had was two wagons, and a bunch of hand carts. Several of them froze to death."

Paul broke down, and cried. "And that ain't the worst of it," he said. He cried for several minutes. Carolyn held him in her arms.

Finally, he continued.

"They didn't have no food, James," he said. "And Jake seen what they had to do to eat and live. They made Jake go down the mountain by himself, and try to get help. It took him over a month to walk through that heavy snow, and get down to the valley. It nearly killed him just doing that. He come running into the bar room one night, crying and screaming like he did a while ago. He finally calmed down, and told me what happened. He wanted to go back up there right then, in the middle of the night. Next day, we got up a rescue party. Jake was just plumb wild, and hysterical to get back up that mountain. There was still a foot of snow on the ground, but we finally got to them."

He paused a moment. James and Carolyn stared at him in shock and disbelief.

"When we got to the camp, it was the most awful thing I've ever seen in my life. I can't even talk about it. And to tell you the truth, I've had lots of nightmares about it myself. But Jake's just gone plumb crazy from it. Sometimes, I can't control him. What am I going to do with him? I can't leave him. If anybody ever needed his friends, he sure does."

"I...I don't know what to say, Paul," James said.

"Paul, let's just take this to the good Lord," Carolyn said. "He knows all about how to take care of Jake."

They let Paul sleep in the parlor. James and Carolyn went back to bed, but they couldn't sleep. Carolyn cried, and James tossed and turned until time to get up.

The news traveled fast. John and Martha came by to check on Jake and Paul. So did Big Jim, Calvin and Malindy, and Patrick and Susan. Bobby and Sarah brought Dr. Morgan.

"Well, I don't think I can help him," Dr. Morgan said. "I know some doctors in Chicago. I may write to them. Maybe they'd know what to do."

"Well, what do we do when he get's like this?" Paul asked.

"Just keep doing what you're doing now," Dr. Morgan said. "Just be his friend. Keep telling him that he's all right, and he's safe. Right now, that's all I know to do."

Big Jim was shaken. He knew Jake Carter was a strong man, and it must have taken something horrible to cause this. He took Paul aside, and demanded an explanation.

Paul told him. Paul relived it every time Jake did, though this experience didn't extract the toll on him it had taken from Jake. Yet his emotions were uncontrollable, and he wept.

Jerry and Sally Connelly brought their children to the boarding house. Sally had heard about Jake, and they also wanted to see James and Carolyn, and all the others.

"James, do you remember me?" Jerry said.

"Hello, Jerry, Sally," he said.

"James, before you say a word, I need to say something," Jerry said. "I'm a changed man, now. I met the Lord, and He saved me. I don't blame you and Carolyn if you don't want me on your property. But we're concerned about Jake, and I just want to see him."

"Well, I'd heard you'd changed, Jerry," he said. "And I'm glad." James extended his hand he'd withheld a moment ago. "Come on in. Jake's still asleep, but Paul's here."

Jerry and Sally were shocked when Paul explained Jake's problem. They prayed with Paul, and he felt better. They prayed for Jake, even though he was still asleep.

Sally visited with Carolyn, Helen and Susan.

"We're thinking about starting a new church over by Salem," Sally said. "We'd love for all of you to come, if you can."

"Sally, I believe you really mean that," Susan said.

"I sure do," Sally said. "We've both changed. Life is so much better now."

When they left, Jerry got Paul to promise he'd let them know if Jake had more problems.

12 BECKY AND BILLY JOE

Martha caught the twinkle in Becky's eyes, and she knew something was in the air. It occurred to her that Becky and Billy Joe just might elope. She didn't mention that idea to anyone, and no one brought it up. But Becky couldn't keep her mind on her studies at all, and she kept making mistakes in subject areas she knew very well. If Jenny knew or suspected any thing, it wasn't evident.

Martha gathered her things, and was ready to leave for home. She looked at Becky for a moment, and started to give her best wishes. Then she decided not to say anything.

Martha came back to the boarding house early the next morning on the pretext of visiting with Carolyn. Sure enough, Becky was gone.

"Has anybody seen Becky?" Jenny said. "She was gone when I got up, and that's not like her."

"Maybe she went back to school a day early," Martha said.

"Martha, she wouldn't leave without me," Jenny said. "Have you seen her, Carolyn?"

"No," she said. "But we get so busy in the kitchen, and we don't always see who comes and goes. I'm sure she's all right."

Martha knew she must speak out. Jenny was getting very worried and upset.

"Jenny, did she say anything about going somewhere today?" Martha said.

"No. Why?"

"Did she take a lot of clothes?"

"I don't know. I didn't look," Jenny said.

Martha and Jenny went to their room. Jenny looked through her sister's dresses.

"She's took out three dresses, Martha. Why would she do that?"

Martha broke into a smile

"Because she's probably eloped with Billy Joe, and most likely they're married by now," Martha said.

Jenny laughed. "That stinker," she said. "I knew she'd been real quiet all day. But it just never dawned on me they'd run off and get married. But I'm glad, though. I think they'll be real happy together."

"What about you, Jenny?" Martha said. "Are things better with you and Charles?"

"Yeah," she said. "It's better, but not completely all right. He got real mad at me for going to that lecture. And when I told him some things Mrs. Young said, he just blew up. We couldn't even talk about it. Anyway, he don't stay mad as long anymore, not like he used to. I still love him, and we're still going to get married."

"That's good to hear," Martha said. "Give him more time, and I believe he'll be all right."

Malindy welcomed Becky and Billy Joe for supper.

"We don't see you much, except for Sunday dinner," Malindy said. "What brings you over tonight?"

"Momma, Daddy, me and Billy Joe got married yesterday," Becky said.

There was hugs and laughter as Malindy and Calvin welcomed Billy Joe to the family.

"We're going to move up to Salem, so we can be close to the school," Billy Joe said. "I got a real good job up there, and we'll get us a place to live tomorrow, when we go back."

Malindy's mind raced ahead. "Honey, you ain't put nothing in that hope chest in years," she said. "Now then, you'll be needing everything. I'll see if I can find you some stuff. Can you take it with you tonight?"

"Yeah, I guess we can," Becky said.

Malindy gave her daughter a little of everything she had. They packed it in the wagon, and Malindy started to cry.

"My babies is all growing up," she said. "Can you all stay tonight?"

"No, Momma," Becky said. "I have to be back to school tomorrow afternoon. But we'll be back Sunday."

A few days later, Malindy came to John's office.

"John, I want you to read this letter, and tell me what you think," she said.

He looked at the letter. The return address was from M. J. Bennett, in Sacramento. He read the letter aloud.

"'Dear Mr. And Mrs. Miller, This is to inform you that your son, Samuel Oliver Miller, has been charged with claim jumping and horse theft. He claims to have no money to hire a lawyer, and wishes to borrow fifty dollars from you. Send the money to him at my address. Thank you. M. J. Bennett, Constable, Sacramento, California.'"

"John, does that say what I think it says?"

"Yes," he said. He took his friends hand. "It accuses him of stealing someone else's gold mine, and stealing horses. That's very serious, and he could be sent to jail for a long time."

Malindy's heart sank.

"I was afraid them boys would get in trouble, and I didn't want them to go," Malindy said. "Calvin ain't seen this letter yet. It'll just about kill him to find this out, like it's killing me now, John."

"Malindy, those gold mining camps are rough and wild," John said. "We didn't want them to go, either. But they're young, and restless. There's nothing any of us could've done to stop them."

"We ain't got that much money, John."

He couldn't tell her about kangaroo courts, crooked attorney's and judges on the take, and many other unethical practices; or that claim jumping often involved the murder of a mine owner. That would only worry her more.

"Let me go talk to the Provisional Government Office," John said. "They can help us find out more about this. I'll ride up there this afternoon."

Malindy thanked him, and went back home.

John felt deeply troubled over Oliver's legal problems. He knew there was more to it than the letter revealed. Calvin and Malindy would be heartbroken, and a young man's future could be ruined.

John explained Oliver's troubles to Mr. Meeker, and asked if the Provisional Government Office could get more information. Mr. Meeker spoke to Dr. McLoughlin , and asked his advice. Then they called on Mr. Peterson for his opinion.

"I think I'd better ride down there, and talk to this Constable Bennett," Peterson said. "I'd better get started in the morning, before the weather gets bad. Say, John, did you hear about that fellow that kind of lost his mind. That sure is awful."

"Yes," John said. "I know Jake, and it is awful. Can you check on Oliver's brother, Johnny Miller? I'm worried about him, too."

When John got back to town, the city was abuzz with news of another wagon train coming down over Mount Hood. In about three days, Oregon City would be accommodating more new settlers. New homes would be built, new businesses would open, and new people would settle into the community.

This always excited John. But today he was worried about his friends. He saw Martha going into the boarding house, and he joined her. She could tell he was troubled. James and Carolyn noticed, also.

"What's wrong?" James said.

"As an attorney, I can't tell you," he said. Just being with his family and friends was a great source of strength for John. Gradually, his spirits lifted, and he felt better.

Patrick and Susan were anxious for the wagon train to arrive. Patrick's mother, Susanna, his brother, Ian and family were on the caravan. It had been six years since they'd seen anyone from Ireland, and there was so much to tell them.

James had built another room on the boarding house, and reserved it for Ian's family. They'd live there until they could build their own home.

The wagons rolled into town, and went about five miles down the road to camp. The wagon master went to Big Jim's office, and gave him the register of names.

Patrick and Susan and the children sat out on the front lawn of the boarding house. They waited and waited for Ian's wagon.

"There they are," Patrick shouted. "Ian, Mother, Coleen, over here," he said.

Ian McDonald pulled his wagon out of line, and stopped at Carolyn's Boarding House. The reunion was joyous, yet bittersweet.

As John came to his office, Little Deer and Morning Dove greeted him. She held a baby in the papoose cradle.

John greeted them, and they came inside.

"Whose baby?" John said.

"Baby's mother dead, don't know where father is," Morning Dove said.

"Some of our braves found her last week," Little Deer said. "We bring her here for Mrs. Greene. Baby's mother Indian, father white man."

"You want Carolyn and James to take the baby?" John said.

"Yes," Little Deer said. "No one in her village wanted to keep baby. My father said you would know what to do."

John knew James and Carolyn would love and care for the baby.

"Let's take the baby over there," he said. "Does the baby have a name?"

Morning Dove shook her head. "They not say," she said. "I call him Boy-Who-Finds-New-Home."

James and Carolyn fell in love with the tiny Indian boy. They called him John James, and the child began to bond with them. Morning Dove gave Carolyn the papoose cradle and blanket. They visited a while, then left for their village.

Patrick and his family visited far into the night. Ian told Patrick the horror of the potato famine, and how many family members and friends who'd died. Coleen and Susan had always been close, and had really missed each other. Susan tried to answer all Coleen's and Mother's questions about the new country she called home. Finally they'd talked it all out, and went to bed.

John told Martha of Oliver's troubles.

"Malindy needs her friend today," he said. "I know from past experience there's more involved than the letter reveals. I just pray that boy didn't kill anyone."

Martha couldn't keep her mind on the school day. She'd forgot to give the younger children their spelling test, and now she was ten minutes over into recess time.

"Children, I'm sorry," she said. "I can't seem to concentrate today. Just play an extra ten minutes."

"Are you all right, Mrs. Campbell?" Billy said.

"Yes, honey," Martha said. "I'm all right. I've just been thinking about something else all day. And thank you for asking."

Martha hugged him, and Billy ran outside to play.

As soon as school was out, Martha hitched up the buggy, and went to see Malindy and Calvin. Malindy was churning butter when she arrived. She stood up to greet Martha, and hugged her with her free arm. She kept churning with the other arm.

Martha felt traces of tears on Malindy's face. It broke her heart to see Malindy so hurt. They talked about Becky and Billy Joe, Jenny and Charles, and Willie and Betty Sue.

"He won't marry till he's got a certain amount of money, or bought him a farm, or something like that," Malindy said. "But I don't know why in the world he'd put it off. She sure is a fine young lady."

They visited for another hour, and Martha realized she needed to get home. Malindy began to weep.

"I don't know what to do about Oliver and Johnny," she said. "They're in trouble, and I can't help 'em."

"I don't know, either," Martha said. "But I know God can help them, and He will, if we just trust Him."

132

"Thank you for coming, Martha," she said. "I'll be all right now. I've got to quit my bawlin', and fix Calvin some supper."

Martha's heart was heavy all the way home.

13 JOHNNY AND OLIVER

Mr. Peterson stopped at John's office. He knocked on the door, and went on in, without waiting for John's answer.

"Mr. Peterson," John said. "I wasn't expecting you for a couple of days yet. How are you?"

"I'm fine, John," he said. "Had a good trip, but I'm pretty upset by what I found."

Oh, no John thought. "What did you find about Oliver?"

"Well, the best we can tell Oliver and this Mr. Monroe argued over who owned a piece of land around Monroe's claim," he said. "The deed Oliver had showed it belonged to him. But on Monroe's deed, it showed the land belonged to Monroe."

"Were there any witnesses to what happened?"

"Yes," Peterson said. "They all agreed Monroe started the fight. He'd filed charges of claim jumping against Oliver, and that started them fighting. Nobody could agree who pulled the gun, but one of them did. They was

134

fighting for the gun, and it went off, and killed Monroe. They all said Oliver jumped on Monroe's horse, and got away. The Constable, this Bennett, caught him four or five hours later, trying to leave town. And that's all I could find out."

"Well, where was Johnny?" John asked.

"I don't know," Peterson said. "I asked Oliver where his brother was, and he said he didn't know."

How will I ever tell Calvin and Malindy? John thought. "Evidently, they've been separated, or Johnny would've helped his brother," he said.

"This Miller family seems to be good people, John," Mr. Peterson said. "Do you know them?"

"Yes, sir, I do know them," John said. "I know them very well. Calvin Miller is one of my closest friends. We came here on the wagon train with them. This is going to just destroy that family. Does Oliver have a lawyer?"

"No. He says he doesn't have any money, and can't hire a lawyer," Peterson said. "He's a stranger in town, a hot headed kid, and nobody will help him."

John knew what he had to do.

He thanked Mr. Peterson, and Peterson left. John walked out the door with him. Mr. Dudley was at Peterson's side immediately. Normally, John would have laughed. But today, it wasn't funny. He locked up his office and went home early.

When Martha got home, she found John packing his trunk.

"John, what are you doing?" she said.

135

John took her hand, and they sat down on the side of the bed. He explained what Mr. Peterson had found. Martha cried.

"I'm going to California, and represent Oliver," he said. "Will you and the kids be all right? I don't know how long this will take. And I've got to find Johnny."

"Yes, we'll be all right," she said.

"Go with me to tell Calvin and Malindy."

"Of course, I will."

Willie and Betty Sue came by to announce they'd be getting married Sunday afternoon, and wouldn't be there for the usual Sunday dinner with the family.

John got right to business.

"Calvin, I need for all the family to set down, and listen for a minute," John said.

They all saw that he was very serious. Malindy began to cry, for she could guess what he'd talk about.

John recapped what Mr. Peterson had told him. The family was stunned.

"I'm going to California, and represent Oliver," John said. "I'll do everything I can for him. I'll find Johnny, and get them back here."

"John, I can't pay you," Calvin said.

"You don't owe me anything," John said. "I owe you more than I can ever repay."

Calvin started to protest further, but John stopped him.

"Just let me do this for you," John said.

The next morning, Willie took John to catch the stagecoach. John was in a hurry, and everything seemed to be moving very slow and awkward. Each day that he couldn't get to those boys caused him great anxiety.

The journey to Sacramento by stagecoach actually took a long time. But John's mind was filled with legal plans and questions. He didn't notice other passengers, or much of the country side. His back was aching from the constant bouncing over the rough dug way roads. He prayed it wouldn't rain until he could get back home. These horrible roads would be even worse if it rained. A few of the roads were post roads, and in much better condition.

The stage arrived in Sacramento on Monday afternoon. John's first order of business was to find Constable Bennett, and visit Oliver. He got off the stage, and stood alone on the wooden sidewalk, with his trunk at his side. He located the Constable's office, and started up the street. But the heavy trunk persuaded him to check into the hotel first. He ate lunch quickly, paid the bill, and left.

John opened the door, and went in.

"Are you Constable Bennett?" he said.

"Yes, I am," he said. "What can I do for you?"

"My name is John Campbell. I'm an attorney for Oliver Miller."

"Come on in, Mr. Campbell," he said. Bennett stood up, and took the keys off the wall. "He's back here in the cell."

John followed him down a dark, dingy hallway to the cell blocks. There were several other men in the cells. They jeered and cursed as John walked by them. The air was stale and rancid, and the stench was sickening. John could barely breathe.

They stopped at a tiny six foot by six foot cell. It was dark and dirty, and cobwebs hung from the ceiling.

"Hey, boy," Bennett said. "You've got company."

"John," Oliver said. "Boy, am I glad to see you. Can you get me out of here? It's awful in here."

"You've got fifteen minutes," Constable Bennett said.

"Are you all right, Oliver?" John said. He took out his notebook and pencil. It was so dark he wasn't sure he'd ever be able to decipher his notes.

"Yeah," Oliver said. "I'm all right."

"Now, you be honest with me. If you're not honest, I won't be able to help you. Now, tell me everything you can remember about that fight."

Oliver began to shake. "I can't stop shaking, John," he said. "Ever since this happened, I just shake like a leaf every time I think about it."

"Oliver, we don't have much time. Now, tell me what you can remember."

"Well, it happened pretty fast," Oliver said. "Monroe, he got real mad at me one morning when I come to work. He told me to get off his property. I said I wasn't on his property."

"Were both deeds recorded by the Land Office here?" John said.

"Yeah. I reckon so."

"Did Johnny own part of your mine? Was his name on the deed, too?" John said.

"No. It was all mine," Oliver said. "Johnny signed on with another big outfit, and they went off out away from here. I stayed here."

"What happened that day?" John said.

"Well, I tried to ignore the old man. But he started pushing me backwards. I fell over something, and I still don't know what that was. But then, he jumped on me, and started hitting me. So, I hit him."

"Did he have the gun?"

"Yeah," Oliver said. "I ain't got no gun, John. You know that. Pa never raised us to be mean to people like that. Oh, God, John. How's Momma? She must be going crazy over this. I never meant for her to find out about it. But they told me I better get me a lawyer. I didn't know what else to do, so, I wrote them."

"They're all right, son," John said. "Now, Oliver, think carefully. Did Monroe try to shoot you?"

"Yeah," he said. "I guess he was trying to kill me. I seen he had the gun, and I was trying to take it away from him. He kept hitting me, and I think he hit me with that gun. I had a big knot on the back of my head for about two weeks, and my head hurt something awful, John. Anyway, I kicked him pretty hard, in the stomach, I think. He hit me again, and I went after him. The next thing I knowed, the gun went off, and he was dead. Did I kill him, John?"

"I don't think so, Oliver," John said. "Did anybody else see the fight?"

"Yeah. Two or three men that worked for Monroe seen the whole thing," he said. "But they're the one's saying that I killed him, and they told that to Constable Bennett."

"I'll go talk to them," John said. "Just one more thing, Oliver. Why did you take Monroe's horse, and run away?"

139

"John, I was scared to death," Oliver said. "I'm still scared to death. Them people's mean, John. I ain't never done nothing like this before in my life. I seen I didn't have a chance, and I just wanted to get away from here."

"Time to go, Campbell," Constable Bennett said.

John walked out of the cell, and Bennett locked the door.

"I'll straighten it out," John said. "You just take it easy. I'll be back to see you tomorrow."

They walked back up the long, dark hallway.

"Can't you put him in a clean cell?" John said.

"Jail ain't for sissies," Bennett said. "He committed a crime. If he's going to act like trash, he'll have to live like trash."

"Where's the Land Office?" John said.

"Two blocks south of here," he said.

"By the way," John said. "Who were the men that witnessed this fight? I need to talk to them."

Bennett provided the list of names, and John went to find them.

John discovered the deed to Mr. Monroe's gold mine had been altered. The deed on file showed three foot less than Monroe was claiming. Monroe had accused Oliver many times of trespassing, but in fact, it was just the opposite. Monroe had encroached three foot onto Oliver's property.

The Assayer's Office confirmed that both mines contained the same vain of gold. John's notes for Oliver's defense began to accumulate.

John's interviews with the three men were also very productive. He'd carefully picked the time and place of each interview, so they could talk in private. They didn't volunteer any information. Then John confronted Mr. Henderson.

"Mr. Henderson," John said. "I believe you knew Monroe took three foot from Oliver's property, didn't you?"

"Well, what if I did know?" he said. "Monroe was nothing but a thief, anyway. But he threatened to kill us, if we told."

"You stood there and watched a grown man beat up on a boy," John said. "Why didn't you try to stop the fight?"

"Like I said–Monroe would've killed me."

"Did Monroe have a gun?" John said.

"Well, yeah. But every man out here's got a gun."

"That boy doesn't. He's never owned a gun in his life," John said.

"Well, nobody ever told me that," Henderson said.

"I will expect you to testify to this in court," John said. "I'll get a court date just as fast as I can."

"What about me?" Henderson said. "If the others think I told, they'll kill me."

"No, they won't," John said. "Come with me."

John took Henderson to Constable Bennett. Henderson told the Constable all he knew.

"Constable Bennett, take this man into custody, and put him in jail," John said. "Keep him away from Oliver. We'll tell the others that he ran away."

Henderson cursed them. "I ain't done nothing. You can't put me in jail. I'm innocent."

"That's a little trick I learned in Boston," John said. "Works like a charm."

The next day, John began searching for Johnny. He asked the Land Office for copies of the mining companies crew manifesto's. He found Johnny listed with the California Mining Company, and the Land Office told him how to find their camp.

John went to the Livery Stable, and saddled a horse. It took most of the morning to locate the camp.

The California gold mines were lawless, and dangerous. There was unchecked drinking, gambling, fighting, and ladies of the evening. This was one of the largest mining operations in the area, and employed a vast number of men. It was also one of the most socially offensive camps.

The girls had their tents lined up along the south edge of the camp. Business was brisk. Several large boulders served as card tables, where games of chance and luck were in session. A nearby still ran at full capacity, and patrons stood in line with their empty jars. There was some pushing, shoving, and name calling, but they remained peaceful.

John found the foreman.

"Excuse me, sir," John said. "Do you have a Johnny Miller working here?"

"Ah, that stupid kid," he said. "Yeah. He used to work with us." He cursed Johnny. "Dumb kid didn't know a thing about dynamite. Some of the men tried to show him how to work with it. But he wouldn't listen. Thought he knowed it all. Well, he knowed it, all right."

"What happened?"

"Well, the boy got drunk," he said. "I've always told my men that what they do on their time off is their business. But when they go to work in that mine," he pointed back to the mine shaft, "you've got to be sober, and keep your mind on your job."

He paused, and spit out tobacco juice, then continued. "The boy went to see one of the girls. Then he went and got falling down drunk. Couple of the men took him down to the creek to sober him up. But they was half drunk theirselves, and they let him come back up here. He checked in, and went to work. He took out some dynamite, and set the charge. But he didn't fix it right. It blowed his arm off, and nearly killed him."

John was visibly shaken. He felt sick.

"They picked him up, and took him to town, to old Doc Butler," the foreman said. "Stupid kid. I should never have hired the boy. Thing of it is, up till then, he'd done a pretty good job. He would've been all right, if he just hadn't got so drunk."

"Well, thank you for telling me," John said. "I'd better go try to find him."

"I hope you luck in finding him," the foreman said. "I liked Johnny. He would've made a good powder monkey. And I'm sure sorry that happened."

They shook hands, and John left. He rode back to Sacramento in despair. By the time he got back to the hotel, John had reached his breaking point. For the next hour, he lay across the bed, crying. John seldom cried. When he did, his soul was in anguish.

"This isn't going to help anyone," John said out loud. He got up and washed his face, and changed clothes. Then he went to find that good café.

He finally located Doc Butler's office. He stood outside for an hour, trying to summon the courage to go in and see Johnny. A light rain began to fall.

Johnny had woke up in Doc Butler's office, screaming in pain. The doctor gave him a white powder in a glass of water. It was hard for him to swallow that dry, bitter stuff, but he got it down.

His ribs were bandaged, and hurting. His head throbbed, and he felt the bandage around his head. His left leg felt as if it were on fire. He could taste blood in his mouth, and his tongue told him two lower front teeth were missing. Then he saw that his left arm was missing, and began to scream again. The horror never ended. He couldn't eat, and the drug induced 'sleep' was worse than no sleep at all.

Doc Butler was a kind, gentle soul. But he was overworked, and couldn't possibly keep up with the needs of his patients. When they brought Johnny in, he was barely alive. He kept trying to tell them what happened. They put pieces of the story together, and figured it out. All Johnny could remember was lighting the fuse. Doc Butler described Johnny's condition to John.

"How bad is it?" John said.

"Pretty bad," he said. "He's made some progress, but he needs a lot more help than I can ever give him."

"I'll pay for anything that boy needs," John said.

"I'm just a simple country doctor, friend," he said. "I don't even know what all that boy needs."

"Can he travel?"

"No, not yet," Doc Butler said. "It may take another month or two before he'll be strong enough to travel. He'll have to walk with a cane from now on."

"I'd like to see him," John said.

"Sure," he said. "But brace yourself. I can't convince him that his left arm's gone. Maybe you can. He says it keeps hurting. But that's impossible."

Johnny was lying in a bed, moaning softly. When they opened the door, he looked up.

"Oh, hi, John," he said. "I'm sure glad to see you. Are we at Fort Laramie yet?"

John couldn't stand to see him like this, yet he knew there was no choice. But something wasn't right, here. Johnny's speech was slow, and slurred. John had heard rumors, and wanted to make sure what he was dealing with.

"What are you giving him for pain?" John said.

Doc Butler showed John the white powder.

John tasted it. "Opium," he said. "I grew up in Boston. I've practiced law there. I've seen too many people die from this stuff. It's dangerous. Where did you get this?"

"There's a lot of Chinamen workers in town," he said. "One of their doctors gave me this. He said to use it for the real bad pain, like what Johnny's got. And it does seem to help. I don't think I could handle Johnny by myself, if it wasn't for this stuff."

145

"Yes," John said. "It can help. But the cure is worse than the pain. Can't you just give him whiskey? Let's try to get him off this."

"Well, I ain't never tried just straight whiskey, but I guess I could."

Johnny woke up briefly, and began mumbling. Soon, he was screaming.

"Momma, there's a spider floating across the room. See it? Over there. Look, I got the gold. They ought to get a new wheel for that wagon. The old one's floating down the river." He drifted back to sleep.

"Doc, I'll set up with him tonight," John said. "You're exhausted. Go upstairs and get some sleep."

"Ah, I'm all right," Doc Butler said.

"No. You're not all right, Doc. You need to rest for about a week. I'll stay here with him," John said.

After Butler went to bed, John located several bottles of whiskey. Every time Johnny woke up in pain, John got him to drink the whiskey. But John knew he couldn't keep doing that, either. He desperately wanted to break Johnny's dependence on the opium, then get him back home. But to do that, he'd need help.

He found writing paper, and wrote a letter to Martha. He detailed the boys circumstances, and asked Martha to describe Johnny's condition to Dr. Morgan. Then she'd ask Willie to bring Dr. Morgan to Sacramento in his most comfortable carriage. He'd meet them at the hotel. John would ask Constable Bennett to send the letter along the post roads.

For the next four days, John and Doc Butler stayed with Johnny day and night. They stayed through the chills, fever, shaking, crying, hallucinations, screaming, and the excruciating pain. John held Johnny's hand to keep him from tearing up the bandages. They tied him to the bed to keep him from getting up, or falling off. Finally, it was over.

"Can I have some more soup?" Johnny said.

Martha cried as she read John's letter. Malindy read it, and they cried together. She talked to Dr. Morgan, and he agreed to meet John in Sacramento.

It took Martha two days to catch up with Willie. She began telling him about his brothers.

"Yeah, I heard about it," he said. "I'm so mad at them, I could just spit nails. Looks to me like they got what they asked for."

"Yes, Willie," she said. "They got into deep trouble. But they're just boys, and they *are* your brothers. If their family and friends don't help them, who will?"

Willie was still mad, and he walked away from the conversation. Martha let him go. She knew he'd think about it, and his family ties would prevail.

14 THE TRIAL

John informed Oliver that his trial would begin Monday morning.

"Now, I want you to shave, comb you hair, and look half way decent," John said. "I'll try to find you some clean clothes. You let me talk for you. Can you do that?"

"Yeah, I guess so," he said. "Can you get me out of here, John? I just want to go home so bad I can't stand it."

"I'm going to do everything I can," John said. "If I can get you out, you'll stay with me. Then we'll go get Johnny."

This was the first time he'd mentioned anything about Johnny. John realized he'd have to prepare Oliver to face Johnny's problems.

"Where is that Johnny, anyway?" Oliver said. "How come he ain't been in here to see me? Me and him's going to have a little talk about this. I would've come to see him every day, if it'd been him instead of me."

"Now, listen to me," John said. "Sit still, and listen." John put his hands on Oliver's shoulders, and gently pushed him down on the side of the bed.

"Johnny got hurt in an accident," John said. He watched Oliver's face contort in grief, as he described Johnny's injuries. "There's no easy way to tell you this, Oliver. He's lost his left arm, and he walks with a limp. The other injuries have healed up pretty good, but he'll never be the same."

Oliver groaned. "Momma was right, John. We shouldn't have come here. Look at us, John. Daddy'll whip us both, and I guess we've got it coming, too. Where…where's he at, John? Can I go see him?"

"As soon as I can get you out of here, we'll go see him," John said. "He's over at Doc Butler's place, across town."

"Does Momma and Daddy know about it?"

"Yes," John said. "I wrote them about you and Johnny. Willie's bringing Dr. Morgan out here to get you and Johnny. They should be here in a few days. Right now, let's concentrate on getting you out of here."

"Is Momma and Daddy all right?" Oliver asked.

"They're all right," John said. "They just want you and Johnny to come home."

"Time to go, Campbell," Constable Bennett said.

Every time John walked through that cell block, it made him physically and emotionally sick. He'd often wondered how anyone could stand being confined in there. Gradually, he began to understand what liberty really is, and what civic responsibility is. He acquired a heightened sense of justice, mercy and compassion. He knew most of the men in that jail were there for a good reason. But he realized there were also those like Oliver. It was impossible to save all of them. But he had a reasonably good chance to help Oliver, and he would give it his all.

John and Constable Bennett walked Oliver out of the cell. Constable Bennett was handcuffed to Oliver. As they passed the other cells, some prisoners spit at them, and cursed them. One man even got his arm through the bars, and grabbed Oliver's arm, causing Oliver to fall, and the Constable to trip over him.

"You get back in there," Bennett yelled. Out came his night stick, and he beat the man's arm until he screamed in agony. He let go of Oliver.

John helped them up. He noticed that Oliver looked sick.

"Are you all right?" John asked.

"Yeah, I'm ok," Oliver said. He began coughing, and he was sweating.

By the time they got outside, Oliver was leaning on the Constable for support. He was glad to sit down in the court room.

"What's wrong with you?" John asked.

"I don't feel good, John," he said.

The judge banged his gavel on the desk, and called the court to order.

"All right, gentlemen, what's this case about?" he said.

Constable Bennett spoke first.

"Your Honor, this man, Samuel Oliver Miller, is accused of claim jumping, and killing a man. I might add that he stole a horse, too."

"What have you got to say for yourself, boy?" the judge asked.

"Your Honor, my client is not guilty of murder. He pleads self defense."

"Constable, do you have any witnesses?" the judge asked.

"Well, no, Your Honor. They didn't show up," Bennett said.

John's spirits rose as high as the heavens.

"Mr. Campbell, do you have any witnesses?"

"Yes, Your Honor. We call Mr. Robert Henderson."

Oliver began coughing. It was a very deep cough, and it hurt his throat and chest. He struggled to stay alert.

John handed the judge a copy of Oliver's deed to the mine, and the copy Monroe had. He explained that Monroe had altered his deed.

Henderson glared at Oliver as he went to the witness stand.

"Mr. Henderson, did Mr. Monroe and Mr. Miller argue about the property lines?"

"Yeah, they argued. Monroe was…"

"Thank you, Mr. Henderson," John said. "How old would you guess Mr. Miller to be?"

"Well, he's just a boy," Henderson said. "Anybody can see that. I'd guess he's about seventeen or eighteen."

"He's fifteen. And how old do you think Mr. Monroe was?" John said.

"I think he was about forty," Henderson said.

"Did you or anyone else in your crew know that Monroe had changed the property lines on that deed?"

"Well, yeah. Me and a couple of other boys watched him do it. He wanted to take Miller's mine, and another one on the other side of his."

"Did Monroe have a gun?" John said.

"Well, yeah. But everybody out here's got a gun."

"Mr. Miller doesn't have a gun. He's never owned a gun in his life. Did Monroe threaten him?"

"Well, yeah, I reckon he did. And he threatened the rest of us if we said anything about it."

"Who started that fight?" John said. "Was it Samuel Oliver Miller, or Mr. Monroe?"

"Monroe started it," Henderson said.

"And the rest of you just stood there and let him beat up a kid?"

"Well, he said he'd kill us, if we done anything," Henderson said.

"Did you see Mr. Miller shoot Mr. Monroe?" John said.

"Well, I…I couldn't tell. They was fighting, and it looked like the boy was trying to take the gun away from Monroe. But Monroe got it back, and the next thing I knowed, it went off, and Monroe was dead."

"So, you didn't see Mr. Miller kill Mr. Monroe, did you?"

"Well, no, I guess not," Henderson said.

"That will be all, Mr. Henderson. Your Honor, the defense rests."

"Constable, do you have anything?" the judge said.

"No," Bennett said.

The judge banged his gavel again.

"Young man, stand up," the judge said.

Oliver coughed again, as he stood. He legs were weak, and he trembled all over.

"Samuel Oliver Miller, this court finds you not guilty of murder. I believe you acted in self defense. You're a free man, Mr. Miller. Court's adjourned."

John's arm went around Oliver to steady him. Constable Bennett came and unlocked the handcuffs.

"No hard feelings, boy," he said. "You seem like a decent kid. Go home, and forget about these gold mines."

"Yes, sir," Oliver said, between coughs.

"John, you're a mighty good lawyer," Bennett said. "Have you ever thought about moving here to Sacramento? We could use a good man like you."

"Thank you, Constable," John said. "But I'm very happy where I am. It's been a pleasure to meet you, sir." They shook hands, and John took Oliver out of the court room as a free man.

The fresh air made Oliver feel better, but that cough persisted.

"Sounds like you need to see Doc Butler," John said.

"No," Oliver said. "I just want to see Johnny, and go home."

"Right now, you're going to see the doctor," John said. "Then you can see Johnny."

By the time they walked to the doctor's office, Oliver was just too weak to protest any more. They went inside, and John rang the cowbell. He heard Doc Butler close a bedroom door.

"Doc, this is Johnny's brother, Oliver Miller," he said. "He's got a real bad cough."

"Any fever, young man?"

"I don't know," Oliver said.

They helped him to a chair. The doctor laid his head on Oliver's chest.

"You've got pneumonia," he said. "I can hear it rattling in both lungs." He felt Oliver's forehead. "Looks like you've got a fever, too."

He turned to John. "Help me get him to bed. I'll see if I can find some medicine for him."

Oliver was coughing so hard that it made his stomach and chest hurt. He leaned on John and the doctor for support.

Johnny had been dozing off and on all morning. He heard the door open, and the deep congested cough. *Sounds like somebody's really sick* he thought. *I probably won't get much sleep tonight.*

As they brought Oliver to the other bed, Johnny looked up, and saw his brother.

"Oh, my God. Oliver, is that you?" Johnny said. He leaped up, and was at his brother's side before they reached the bed.

Oliver collapsed into Johnny's embrace. They both began to cry, and Oliver coughed until he was hurting again.

Doc Butler took control.

"Oliver, you've got to get in the bed, right now," he said.

Johnny was shocked to see his brother so desperately ill. He stepped back, and let John and Doc Butler help Oliver in bed.

"John, what on earth happened to him?" Johnny said.

While Doc Butler attended to Oliver, John took Johnny aside, and told him about Oliver's problems.

"Now, both you boys get some rest," Doc Butler said. "You can visit later."

"Yes, sir," Oliver said.

The brothers spent a restless night, as they coughed and talked. Finally, Doc Butler fixed them both a warm toddy so they'd go to sleep and leave him alone. By morning, the fever had broken, and Oliver felt a little better.

Willie and Dr. Morgan arrived on Thursday. John met them at the stage depot, and took them to the hotel. He filled in the details as fast as he could.

Willie still felt a twinge of anger at his brothers. He actually wanted to spank them. But they were counted as grown men, now, and responsible for their own actions. He wished they had listened to the good advice that was given to them. But he knew it would do no good to yell at them now. He remembered the many times on the wagon train when he'd been so head strong. *I didn't listen to Daddy, either. So I guess I can't get after them too much* he thought.

"Willie, I want to talk to you," John said. "Before we go in there, there's some things you need to know."

John described Johnny's injuries, Oliver's pneumonia and legal troubles, and the need to get them back home safely.

Both boys were eating lunch when they arrived. John and Dr. Morgan went in first, and Willie was behind Dr. Morgan. Willie didn't know what to say to them, and almost dreaded to see them. They walked to the foot of Oliver's bed before Willie stepped out in the open.

Willie was horrified at Johnny's disabilities. He could scarcely walk from one bed to the other, and the empty shirt sleeve hung loosely at his side. When Johnny saw them, he bounded out of bed, and ran to Willie.

Willie had extended his hand, but Johnny ran past the handshake, and hugged him.

"Take us home, Willie," Johnny said.

"Now, hold it, both of you," Doc Butler said. "Neither one of you is able to go anywhere. You need to rest a few more days."

"I agree with him," Dr. Morgan said. "We've got to let you get a little better, before we go back home."

Willie was still speechless. He didn't want to stare at the empty shirt sleeve, and he didn't know how to begin a conversation.

Johnny spoke first.

"Willie, did Bobby get them cows home?"

"He sure did," Willie said. He told about the cattle drive, and the cheese plant they were preparing.

"What about Becky and Billy Joe?" Oliver said.

Willie told them all the latest news from the family and friends.

"Well, tell them the rest of it," Dr. Morgan said.

Willie's face got red.

"Me and Betty Sue got married."

"Doc, when can we go home?" Oliver said.

"Well, I'd say in a couple of days, if you both do all right."

Doc Butler could see the tiredness in their face's.

"Well, I think it's time we let these boys rest," he said. "They can come back tonight and see you."

John and Willie went to the General Merchandise store. They bought Oliver and Johnny new clothes and shoes. They purchased several things for the families back home.

"John, I can't stand to see them like this," Willie said. "I was so mad at them, when you wrote and told us what happened. But seeing them sick and hurt has just tore me up. How in the world is Johnny ever going to make a living? What kind of work can a one-arm man do, anyway?"

"You'd be surprised what a one-arm man can do, when he sets his mind to it," John said. "Right now, they just need to get well. They'll need their family and friends to be there, and help them when we can."

15 HOMECOMING

The cold November rain poured for two days. The roads and streets were muddy, but Johnny and Oliver didn't care. This was the day they were starting home, and nothing would deter them.

"I wish you would wait til it stops raining," Dr. Morgan said. "This'll be hard on both of you. I don't have very much medicines to help you."

"I agree with him," Doc Butler said.

"No," Johnny said. "We're leaving right now, soon as Willie and John get here."

Dr. Morgan just shook his head. "Still impatient, ain't you? I know you want to get back home, and I don't blame you for that."

Willie drove his coach up to the door of Doc Butler's office. John helped him get the bags on board, then Doc Butler brought Johnny and Oliver out, and helped them get in.

"Doc, I sure want to thank you for taking good care of me," Johnny said. "Don't know what I would've done without you."

They shook hands, and Johnny got in the coach.

Oliver thanked Doc Butler, and got in. He sat down between John and Dr. Morgan.

"You boys take care of yourselves," Doc Butler said. "If you're ever back in town, come by and see me."

Willie closed the door, and climbed up to the drivers seat. He started the team, and drove north.

The rain kept falling. Willie was soaking wet, but he didn't care. His emotions were so mixed. He was still just a little angry with his brothers, yet his heart was breaking for them. The rain and tears seemed to wash away his anger, and he began to feel compassion and forgiveness.

The 'roads' were a nightmare of mud and potholes. The coach got stuck several times. John, Dr. Morgan and Willie had to push and pull it out. Johnny and Oliver wanted to help, but they were told to just stand aside. By the end of the day, Johnny was in severe pain again. They slept in the coach that night.

The next day, the sun was shining, but it was much cooler.

Malindy heard the coach drive up. The maternal heart knew it was her children.

I can't cry in front of 'em she thought. *No matter how bad it is, I just can't cry now.*

Dr. Morgan had to help Johnny into the house. His back and legs had been hurting since the day they left Sacramento. He wanted to get home with no more delays, so he never complained. He knew they could tell he was in pain. The limp was very pronounced, even with Dr. Morgan's help.

They all tried to get through the door at once, and Oliver almost knocked down Dr. Morgan and Johnny. Willie and John brought their things inside.

When Malindy saw them, the tears came anyway. She held them both for a long time, and struggled to hold back her runaway emotions. At last, she could let go of them.

"I'm so glad you're both home," was all she could say.

Willie gave her a quick hug. "I'll come back tonight, and visit with everybody," he said.

Dr. Morgan led Johnny to a chair.

"Now, I want to see both you boys at my office in a couple of days," he said. "Malindy, keep them warm, and make sure they get some rest."

Malindy prepared lunch. Calvin would be home soon, and she knew the boys were hungry, too. She fried some ham, made potato soup and biscuits.

"Hey, Ma, save me a wad of that starter dough," Oliver said. "I'll show you how to make sourdough bread. It's really good, and you'll all like it."

"Sourdough bread?" she said. "Why, I ain't never heard of such a thing. Where did you get that?"

"In Sacramento," he said. "That's what they use in all them mining camps."

Malindy gave him a lump of the dough. Oliver wrapped the dough in an old pillow case, then tucked it under his shirt, and sat back down.

"What in the name of common sense are you doing that for?" Malindy said.

"Well, I've got to keep it warm," he said.

"Then put it over here, on the far side of the hearth," Malindy said. "It'll stay warm there."

"But in California, we had to sleep with this ball of dough to keep it warm. The cook done that every night," Oliver said.

"Honey, this ain't California," Malindy said gently. "Just put it down there on the hearth. I raise all my dough there."

Reluctantly, Oliver placed the dough on the hearth.

John couldn't wait to get home. Many nights he'd dreamed of Possum Hollow, and the comfort of that warm fireplace, with Martha and the children beside him. He missed his family. But knowing they'd be waiting for him gave him encouragement to return home.

Willie stopped the coach, and John got out. He paid Willie, and got his trunk down.

"Thank you, Willie," John said. "Possum Hollow sure looks good." Willie drove off, and John opened the gate.

Martha and the children were down at the hen house, gathering eggs. When she heard the coach, and John's voice, she put the eggs down. She picked up Carolyn, took Johnny's hand and they ran to meet John.

John and Martha sat up late, and he told her all the things he saw in California.

"You did the right thing," she said. "And I'm proud of you."

The weather turned cold and windy. Snow clouds spit their icy particles of snow and sleet. Calvin and John filled Malindy's smokehouse with meats, then filled Martha's smokehouse. Next, they would help James. Since that was for the boarding house, it took a very large supply.

161

Oliver and Johnny had found the pants in Sacramento. They were made of a tent-like material, and were long lasting and comfortable. John and Willie had purchased some, too. Each of them began wearing these new pants as the weather got colder. Calvin wanted some, but Malindy said they looked silly. Who would wear a tent?

Johnny had been very quiet since coming home. He never talked about his experiences with the mining crew, in fact, he wouldn't talk much at all. Today, he needed to test himself.

He took an axe, and Calvin's extra rifle and bullets, and went to a clearing in the woods. He found a small sapling, and began chopping it. He tried to swing the axe in the same manner as one would if using two hands. But the chopping motions were wild and erratic. He was afraid he might cut his legs with the axe.

Johnny stepped back, and thought for a moment. Then he stood to one side, and changed the angle of the swing. It didn't take long to cut down the tree. He chopped it into usable lengths of firewood. From the branches, he made a crude sled to haul the wood home. Then he decided to cut a bigger tree. Johnny worked until the pain became so intense he had to stop.

As he rested on the tree stump, a turkey gobbled near the edge of the clearing. Johnny found the rifle. He cocked the trigger, and fired. The bird flew away unharmed.

Johnny arranged sticks and branches at various heights for target practice. At first, he couldn't hit any of them, but he persisted until his aim improved. When he had only two bullets left, he headed for home.

Malindy was surprised to hear wood being stacked in the wood pile. She looked out, and saw Johnny measuring the rick of wood. She wanted to go help him, but realized he needed to do this himself.

He'll make it she thought. *With the good Lord's help, my boy'll make it.*

16 FRIENDS

Martha and the children stopped by to visit everyone at Carolyn's Boarding House. It had been several days since she'd seen Carolyn, and she needed that bit of comfort she always found here.

Carolyn took the baby, while Johnny went to play outside with the McDonald children. He had made friends with Michael, Ian and Coleen's son.

"I'll make us some tea," Carolyn said. "I know how much you like it. We haven't had a good visit in a long time. What's been going on at your house?"

As they talked, James came in. He threw his hat across the room. It hit the peg on the wall that held coats and hats, then fell to the floor. Usually, he was able to throw the hat onto the peg, and it would stay in place.

"Huh," James grunted.

"What's wrong, dear?" Carolyn said.

"Oh, it's Johnny," he said. "He sold me some wood. But he won't let me help him unload it, or rick it up. I can tell he's hurting so bad he can hardly move."

Johnny came in, and James paid him.

"Hello, Johnny," Martha said. "How've you been?"

"Hi, Martha," was all he said. "James, I'll keep your wood supplied every week." He put the money in his pocket, and left.

Martha cried. This was the first time she'd seen Johnny since he came home.

"He's determined to do everything by himself," James said. "Up to a point, I can understand. But sometimes, we all need a little help."

The children came running in.

"Momma, what happened to Johnny's arm?" Johnny said.

"He lost his arm in an accident," she said. Martha smoothed out his tasseled hair.

"If he lost it, maybe we could help him find it," Johnny said.

"I don't think so, honey," Martha said. "We can't ever get his arm back."

"You mean he has to stay like that forever?"

Martha nodded.

"Boys, how would you like to help me bring some of that wood into the kitchen? They'll need it to cook today."

The boys and James carried wood to the kitchen wood bin, then to the dining room fire place.

"You know, I believe Paul Smith is serious about Miss Molly," Carolyn said. "They've been keeping regular company now for about three weeks."

"But what about Jake?" Martha said. "Who's going to look out for him?"

"Well, Molly calls him 'Uncle Jake'," Carolyn said. "I don't think Jake has anything to worry about."

This news pleased Martha very much.

"And I heard that Patrick and Ian are going to start a freight hauling business," Carolyn said. "In fact, Susan says that's all they talk about, now."

"My friends are all doing well," Martha said. "And I see your babies are energetic, too."

"I don't know what we'd do without Jane and John James," Carolyn said. "They're such a part of our lives, now. We want to adopt them."

"Yes, John told me," Martha said. "He said the Provisional Government Office will help with the adoption."

Calvin and Malindy came by for a short visit. They were on their way to Jenny and Charles' wedding in Salem.

"Johnny brought us some wood a while ago," Carolyn said. "Looks like he's doing good."

"Well, I guess he's all right," Malindy said. "He won't talk to nobody. He ain't said half a dozen words to me since he got home."

"James said he wouldn't let him help unload the wood, or rick it up," Carolyn said.

"Yep. He can sure be stubborn," Malindy said. "That boy come a hair-spat of getting his self plumb killed, and he won't let nobody do nothing for him."

Susan, Helen and Coleen came out of the kitchen. They sat down to visit a while.

"Carolyn, we're out of sausage," Helen said. "What do you want us to fix for breakfast, now?"

"Oh, dear," Carolyn said. "I'll have to see if I can buy it somewhere. Just use bacon in the morning."

"Have you got any black-eyed peas?" Malindy said.

"Yes, there's a big barrel full," Susan said.

"Well, let me show you how to make sausage out of them," Malindy said.

Everyone's interest was piqued.

"Malindy, how in the world can we do that?" Carolyn said.

"My Momma showed me how to do that when I was a little bity thing," Malindy said. "It's real easy. You just cook the peas, and mash them up. Then stir in all the flour, sage and spices that we put in good sausage. Shape it into them little patties, and fry it. Tastes just like sausage. They'll never know the difference."

"I've got to see this to believe it," Martha said..

"Girls, go cook me some black-eyed peas, and I'll prove it to Miss Smarty-Pants here," Malindy said.

The aroma of good food filled the house. They laughed and talked, as good friends always do. When it was time to prepare the 'sausage', they all crowed into the kitchen to watch Malindy's handiwork.

"Here, Martha," Malindy said. "Taste this."

Martha was astonished.

"This does taste like sausage," she said. "And it's really good. You're still the most amazing woman I know."

"Carolyn, I've been thinking," Helen said. "If you and James had a cow, some chickens, and a couple of hogs, you'd have your own food supply. Then you wouldn't have to buy so much."

"You know, you're right, Helen," she said. "I'll talk to James about it. I don't know why we didn't think about this."

John delivered the divorce papers to Paul Smith. Paul was anxious to get on with his life.

"I'll sign the papers right now," Paul said. "Me and Molly's getting married, and I'll be free of Mary. She won't have no claim on me now." His hands were sweaty, and left smudges on the papers, but that was all right. Now Paul was a free man.

"I should have done this a long time ago, John," he said. "But I loved her, and I kept thinking after a while, she'd come to her senses."

John walked back to his office, and greeted Arthur Kelly.

"Hello, Arthur," John said. "Come on in, and visit a while."

"John, I hear you're a California lawyer now," Arthur said. "I hear you defended that Miller boy *pro bono*. You know that'll make a good story back home. So, tell me about it, John."

John really didn't like to talk about himself very much, and it was somewhat difficult for him. Arthur had to dig out the information, but got enough details for a very good article.

"John, I need to talk to you off the record," Arthur said. "I have to confess something, and this is not easy for me, but I must tell you."

John wondered if Arthur had done something questionable, but couldn't believe him capable of wrong doing.

"John, I came here with a preconceived opinion of you and Martha," Arthur said. "Adam Campbell and Charles Montgomery talked my editor into sending me on this trip. Charles and Adam paid my expenses out here. My editor wanted the stories, and they wanted me to discredit you and Martha."

"I suspected as much," John said.

Arthur continued. "After I met you and Martha, and got to know you, my opinions of you changed. The stories I've sent back to Boston reflect the real John and Martha Campbell. I found that I couldn't write the negative articles they hoped I'd write. I've come to respect and admire you both, and I hope you'll consider me as your friend. I'm very sorry that I fell for such a scheme, John, and I ask you to forgive me, if you can."

John shook his hand. "I'm sorry you got caught up in this," he said. "Arthur, you're a good man, and I'm proud to call you my friend."

"I may not have a job when I get back home," Arthur said.

"There are other newspapers, Arthur," John said. "I'll be glad to write a letter of recommendation. Let me know if you need it."

"Thank you, John," Arthur said.

Big Jim received the news early that morning. Aunt Susie had died. Jerry and Sally had went to check on her. She told them where to find her will. They stayed with her til the end.

"Jim, she said to give this to you," Jerry said. "She told us it was her will. We haven't opened it, because she wanted you to do that."

Jim took the envelope, opened it, and silently read it.

"When's the funeral?" Jim asked.

"We'll bury her tomorrow," Jerry said.

After the funeral, Jerry, Sally, Henry and Minnie gathered around Big Jim. He took out the envelope.

"'To my children,'" Jim began. "'I don't have much to give you, but I want you to have some things. I want Jerry and Sally to have half of my land, and Henry and Minnie get the other half of my land. Sally and Minnie get everything in the house. Divide it between them, Jim. Now, all of you, just remember to live like I showed you, and trust in the Lord.'"

They talked quietly for a few minutes, then went home.

The next week, Paul and Molly were married. Paul had asked about the old Pearson farm. He found that the land had been abandoned, so he filed a deed to the land. They moved in the cabin, and Paul began building a cabin for Jake.

17 WHEELS AND DEALS

Oregon City was alive with business and commerce. New homes and businesses were coming each day. New settlements were starting up all along the Willamatte River. This brought the need for more workers.

Willie had thought about this venture for a long time. If he could get Patrick and Ian, Johnny and Oliver to join him, they would control the freight and passenger trade from Oregon City up to Portland.

"Look, fellows," Willie said. "If the five of us go in together, we can control the whole thing. I can use my coaches for the passengers to and from Portland, Johnny and Oliver can take my routes here. Then Patrick and Ian can handle the wagon and barge freight. We won't have to buy any new wagons, or barges. We can use what we've already got. How 'bout it?"

"Well, yes," Ian said. "I can handle the barge freight. I don't know a thing about the wagons, though."

"I can take the freight wagons," Patrick said.

171

"I ain't got no money," Johnny said.

"I don't either," Oliver said. "How much do you want for them wagons of yours, Willie?"

"Make me a down payment of what ever you can," Willie said. "Then pay me a little along the way till you get it paid for."

Johnny was sullen.

"I don't want no handout," he said.

"This ain't a handout," Willie said. He was getting irritated with his brother's pride. "I know you ain't got enough to buy the wagons outright, and I didn't ask you to do it that way. Just pay me what you can, when you can."

"Let me think about it," Johnny said.

"Don't take too long," Willie said. "Tell me pretty soon, and we'll go talk to John, and make it all legal and right."

"Count me in," Patrick said.

Ian and Oliver agreed.

By the end of the week, John had the papers ready. They all met in his office on Friday morning, and signed their names to The Miller-McDonald Wagon Company. Johnny reluctantly signed on as partner in the deal.

Willie needed more horses now. He decided to ask Jake and Paul if they'd like to help.

"Jake, where's the best place to get good horses?" Willie said.

"Well, there's plenty of wild horses," Jake said. "But you'd have to break them to ride, and pull a load."

"Can you and Paul do it?" Willie said.

"Yeah, I guess we could," Jake said. "But I think I'm getting a little too old to be breaking horses. Paul would have to do that. How many do you want?"

"About a dozen."

"We'll see what we can do," Jake said.

Dr. McLoughlin, Mr. Peterson and Mr. Meeker came to see John Monday morning. They visited for a few minutes, and caught up on all the pleasantries.

"John, I'll get right to the point," Dr. McLoughlin said. "We all think you're the best lawyer in the territory, and we need you. We'd like you to help write the legislation for Oregon statehood."

John didn't know what to say. He felt deeply honored, and humbled by this mind-boggling task.

Mr. Meeker picked up the conversation.

"We've grown to the point where we need the protection of Washington," he said. "After what happened to the Whitman's last year, if we want more people to come out here, then we have to offer them better protection. All we've got now is this Provisional Government Office, and that's just not enough."

"John, remember Pauline Edwards?" Mr. Peterson said. "Look at the problems you ran into with that–you couldn't defend her very well, and we couldn't lock her up very well. And there's been two or three other murders up around Portland since then. We just don't have good organized territorial laws. And we're growing so fast the Provisional Government Office can't keep up. Besides, it doesn't have any teeth in the law, anyway."

173

"How 'bout it, John? Will you help us?" Mr. Meeker said.

"What about my practice here?" John said. "I can't just walk out and leave my clients. I'll have to think about this, gentlemen."

"We understand that," Dr. McLoughlin said. "We're prepared to compensate you for your time. You let us know how much your time is worth for, say one week's legal work, and we'll pay you."

"When do you need an answer?" John said.

"Come up to my office Thursday or Friday," Mr. Meeker said. "We'll work out more details then."

John agreed, and shook their hands. Dr. McLoughlin stood up, and put his hat on. John wondered what he'd gotten himself into.

"John, we have all confidence that you can handle the job," Dr. McLoughlin said. "If I didn't think you could, I'd never ask you."

"We'll see you in a few days," Mr. Meeker said.

As they walked out the door, Councilman Dudley pounced on them. John could hear him expounding the goodness of his wife's 'prize-winning apple pie'.

The first thing I'm going to do is make Mrs. Dudley's pies illegal John thought. *That would do more to help the Oregon Territory than anything else I can think of.*

John stopped to tell James and Carolyn about this new adventure.

"Looks like you'll get a political career, after all," James said.

"No, no," John said. "I don't want anything to do with politics. But I think I do want to help write this legislation. Just think what a marvelous opportunity this is."

"I know you can do it, John," Carolyn said. She gave him a gentle hug. "Does Martha know yet?"

"No," John said. "I'll tell her as soon as I get home. And, please don't say anything about this till I get things worked out."

"It's safe with us, John," James said.

John did his evening chores as fast as possible. He couldn't wait to tell Martha about this offer from the Provisional Government Office.

"Where's the fire, John?" Martha said.

His face lit up.

"Martha, you'll never guess... I mean, it sure surprised me. I still can't believe it..."

"Well, what? What surprised you? What is it you still can't believe?"

"Oh, I'm sorry," John said. "It's just that I haven't been this excited about anything in a long time. Dr. McLoughlin, Mr. Meeker and Mr. Peterson have asked me to help write the legislation for Oregon statehood. What do you think about that, Martha?"

Martha gasped. "John, that's wonderful," she said. "When do you start?"

"I don't know. Right now, I guess," he said. "I'm going to see Mr. Meeker on Thursday, and we'll talk more about it then. I don't have any idea where to start. There's so many things that need to be done. We'll have to set priorities, and I just don't know what all we'll have to do."

Martha and the children said good night to John. They went off to bed, while he began pouring over his law books.

The next day, Martha found it hard to concentrate on helping Becky and Jenny with their studies. The girls were having problems with Latin again.

"Girls, just calm down," Martha said. "We'll get through this. But I can tell right now what your problems really are."

"Oh, really?" Jenny said.

"Yes," Martha said. "Your problem is still Charles. I thought you two had settled everything. What is it now?"

"He expects me to cook his meals, wash his clothes, and go help him take care of them stupid fruit trees," Jenny said. "Then I'm so tired, I don't feel like studying. He ain't keeping his word. He's suppose to do all that, and let me study."

"Now Jenny," Martha said sternly. "You put your foot down. Tell him in no uncertain terms that you need time to study first, then you'll help him. Will you do that?"

"Yeah, I guess so," Jenny said. "But what about Becky? She's sick all the time."

"I think I know what's wrong with her, too," Martha said. "Becky, have you told your mother yet?"

Becky began to laugh, and shook her head. Jenny gasped, and hugged her sister. They laughed and cried until Becky got sick, and had to be excused. When she returned, Martha shared John's exciting new job. Then they returned to the study of Latin.

18 WILD HORSES

John whistled a tune, as he went to Mr. Meeker's Provisional Government Office. He was excited and scared at the same time. When he entered the office, the others were already there. Arthur Kelly greeted him, also.

"Congratulations, John," Arthur said. "I know you'll be exceptionally good at this job."

John didn't want to tell him not to print a story on his mission here, but he wished Arthur would just set on it. He knew Arthur would give this story a front page by-line. But he pushed his thoughts aside, and sat down with the others to start this most serious business.

"John, we'd like you to work one or two weeks each month," Dr. McLoughlin said. "Do you have the figures ready for your compensation?"

John handed him the paper listing his needs, and expenses. Dr. McLoughlin passed it to the others, and they all seemed satisfied.

"I believe we all agree, John," he said. "This seems fair and honest. If you have more expenses than what's listed here, or need more salary, please let us know."

The meeting adjourned later that afternoon. Mr. Meeker gave John a trunk full of official records, law books, city business records for all the settlements, land transactions and deeds, marriage and divorce records, birth and death records, city government records for Oregon City and Portland, and what looked like a ton of other papers.

"Oh, I almost forgot," Mr. Meeker said. "Here's the Provisional Government records. Now, you'll need to go through all these, and come up with a list of things to do first."

John stared in disbelief. How could anyone ever find the time to read all these things?

Arthur picked up one end of the trunk, and John took the other end. Mr. Peterson held the door open for them, and they went outside.

"Where's your wagon?" Arthur said.

"Well, it's over at the Livery Stable," John said. "I never thought I'd have to carry anything. I'll go get it."

The stage coach from Portland arrived at four that afternoon. Mary Smith got out, and took her bags. She paid Willie, and he drove away.

Little smart-alec don't even remember me Mary thought. The first order of business would be a place to live, then worry about a job later. She'd accumulated a tidy sum of money anyway, and could live comfortably for a very long time.

I wonder where my Paulie is she thought. Mary had a score to settle with her husband, Paul. It would be interesting to see his reactions. *I'll teach that little picayunish varmint not to pull foot and leave me.*

Mary stopped at the first boarding house she saw, and got a room. She was tired, and just wanted to rest tonight.

John had talked Arthur into coming home with him tonight. He really wanted Arthur to help him carry in that mountain of papers.

"Martha, it's good to see you again," Arthur said. "Something smells wonderful."

"Thank you," Martha said. "I hope you like my corn pudding and roast venison. I would've made something special, if I'd known you were coming."

John, Arthur and Johnny finished the evening chores, and came inside just as Martha got the meal ready.

"Martha, you're an amazing woman," Arthur said.

Martha laughed. "No, Arthur," she said. "I'm not the least bit amazing. It's women like Malindy, Carolyn, Helen, or Susan and Coleen that are amazing. You should write stories on them, Arthur."

"I'm thinking about returning to Boston," Arthur said. "My 'expense account' is almost depleted now. I have just enough left to get home. Are there any messages either of you would like me to deliver in Boston?"

"Well, I hadn't even thought of that," Martha said.

"When are you leaving?" John said, as he passed around the cornbread.

"I have several stringer articles I'm writing for Mr. Peterson," Arthur said. "When those are finished, I'll probably leave then."

"We'll see you before then, I trust," Martha said.

"Martha, if you ever get back to Boston, there's a lady you should meet," Arthur said. "She's very active in the suffrage movement, and her husband pastors a large church in Boston. Look me up when you get there, and I'll introduce you."

"I will," Martha said.

After the meal, Martha cleaned her posts and pans, while Arthur played with the children. John wanted to get started on that voluminous stack of paper.

"What on earth is all this?" Martha said.

John explained his work load, and it's importance.

"I though I'd better get started," he said.

"Surely you don't intend to read *all* that tonight, do you?"

"No," he said. "But I can make a little headway on it."

Paul and Jake found a herd of wild horses. They'd built a temporary corral, and began bringing them in.

Jake had been doing much better. He was regaining his confidence and strength, and there'd been no nightmares for several weeks now. He began to actually enjoy rounding up these horses. Jake showed Paul how to 'talk' to the horses with his hands, eyes, mannerisms, the rope, and his voice. He explained how to use the corral for more than just confinement of the animals. Finally, he thought Paul was ready to try on his own.

"Now, remember what I told you," Jake said. "You got to tell this horse that you're the boss, and you ain't going to hurt him. But he's got to do what you tell him, then reward him when he does it right. Never mistreat him, never break his spirit, and we'll have a fine bunch of horses."

Paul climbed over the fence, and stood looking at the big brown horse. He was a beautiful animal, strong and proud. The horse snorted. Paul stood still, and made eye contact with the horse. He snorted again, and shook his head. The 'talking' began in earnest. Finally, he was able to speak verbally to the horse, ever so gently. Soon he was gaining the horse's confidence and trust. He extended his hand to touch the stallion's face. The horse whinnied nervously, and suddenly reared up on his hind legs, pawing the air. Paul jumped back.

"Easy, easy," Jake said.

The process was repeated three more times. By evening, Paul was petting the horse. By the next evening, Paul had the bit and bridal on him. Then he began leading the horse.

"See if you can get a saddle on him in the morning," Jake said.

Big Jim thought he was seeing things. *Is that Mary Smith?* he thought.

"Mary, Mary Smith," Jim said.

She turned around to see who'd called her.

"I should've knowed it was you," she said. She saw his badge. "You're the Sheriff?"

"Yep, I sure am," he said. "What are you doing here, Mary?"

"Well, I come here to see Paul, if that's any business of yours," she said.

"It ain't my business, unless it gets ugly like it used to," he said. "But he may not want to see you."

"Oh, yes, he will," she said, with the utmost confidence. "I'm his wife. He'll see me. Now, where is he?"

"Mary, don't you do this," Big Jim said. "Paul got divorced from you, and he's remarried. Now, you leave him alone."

"He done what?" she screamed. Her face turned red, and she stomped her foot. "When did he do that?"

"I don't know exactly–sometime back in the summer, I reckon," Jim said.

"Well, nobody ever told me anything about it," she shouted. "Where's he at, Jim?"

"Mary, I'm not about to tell you where he's at," Big Jim said. "You sure ain't changed a bit. If you come here, and start something with them, I'll run you out of here, just like I kicked you off the wagon train."

"You quit your threatening me, Jim Cross," she said. "I ain't done nothing wrong, and you can't push me around like that. Now, you tell me where he's at, and what's her name."

"I'm not going to tell you nothing, Mary," he said. "You just simmer down, and leave them alone."

"Well, if you won't tell me where he's at, I'll just find somebody who will," she said.

People were staring at them, and it embarrassed Big Jim. Mary was undaunted.

"Why didn't somebody notify me about this so-called divorce?" she said.

"Because nobody knowed where you were," Jim said. "Now, calm yourself down, before I have to arrest you."

"Don't you lay a hand on me, Jim Cross," she said. "Now, I want to know where my Paulie is."

Before he could answer, Councilman Dudley appeared out of nowhere.

"My goodness, what's all this balderdash about?" he said. "I could hear your arguments all the way up to my house." He removed his hat, and bowed gracefully to Mary. "Ma'dam, may I help you?"

"Yes, you certainly may," Mary said. "At last, here's a gentleman who's willing to help a lady."

"*You* sure ain't no lady," Big Jim said. "Mr. Dudley, this don't concern you at all. Now, you go back home, and stay out of this. Do you understand me?"

"But Sheriff, I just wanted to help."

"Yes, he's a nice man, and I need his help."

"Shut up, Mary."

"But Jim, I left you one of the wife's best apple pies in your office. I thought you might like it."

"You get that thing out of my office before I shoot you," Big Jim shouted.

By now, half the town was listening.

"Sir, do you know Paul Smith? I need to find him."

"Mary, I told you to hush," Jim said. "Mr. Dudley, you go back home, right now, or I'll arrest you."

"Well, you don't have to be so uppity about it," Mr. Dudley said. "I was just trying to help this nice lady." He started walking toward his home.

"She don't need your help," Jim yelled.

"Yes, I do, sir," Mary said.

"Mary, so help me, you're under arrest for... for disturbing the peace," Jim said.

"Me? Disturbing the peace? I did not. You're the one that started this argument, cause you won't tell me where Paul is. I ain't done nothing. What are you arresting me for?"

Big Jim jerked her down the street, and shoved her through the door to the jail. He slammed the jail door, and threw the keys in his desk drawer. Then he took Mr. Dudley's pie, and threw it out into the street. He was so mad he was shaking all over.

"Jim, you let me out of here," Mary said. "I know a good lawyer up there in Portland, and I'm going to tell him about this."

Big Jim slammed the door, and began walking toward Carolyn's Boarding House. Helen was mopping the kitchen floor when he came in. She knew something was wrong.

"I need to talk," Jim said. They went out to the back porch, and sat down. Big Jim poured his heart out to his best friend and wife.

Two hours later, Big Jim came back to his office.

"All right, Mary," he said. "I'll let you out of here, if you'll promise to leave Paul alone."

"Oh, all right," she said.

"Now Mary," Jim said. "If Paul wants to see you, he'll come by and talk. Otherwise, just let the man alone. And keep yourself out of trouble."

Jake and Paul had twelve horses broke to ride and pull a load. They brought them back to Paul's pasture. Paul was glad to be home, and settled back into the routine life he longed for.

Jake was very pleased. Paul had learned well, and Jake was proud of him. They made a good team, Jake and Paul. Life was beginning to look brighter for Jake.

They delivered the horses to Willie's stable early Monday morning.

"You boys done a good job," Willie said. "I sure like that big brown stallion there. I want him for the lead on my best coach."

Willie paid them, and Jake started for home. Paul walked over to the big brown horse.

Paul petted his face and head, and the horse snorted a little. "You behave yourself," Paul told him. "And keep the others in line, too. I'll see you ever once in a while." The horse shook his head, and twitched his ears. Then he pushed Paul away with his nose, as if to say *Go on home. I'll be just fine.*

As Paul approached his cabin, he heard people shouting, and wondered what was going on. He saw a strange buggy in the yard, and Jake and Molly were yelling at some woman. The dog barked a friendly welcome, but they never stopped arguing.

"What in tarnation is going on here?" Paul said.

Mary turned to face Paul, and threw herself at him. Paul staggered backward, and grabbed the porch rail for support.

"Oh, Paul, honey, I'm so glad to see you," Mary said. "Nobody would tell me where you were for the longest time, til that nice Mr. Dudley told me last night."

"Mary, what in the world are you doing here?" Paul said. "You…you can't stay here."

"You sure can't stay here," Molly said. She grabbed Mary's arm, and pulled her away from Paul.

Mary responded by slapping a stinging blow to Molly's face. The red imprint of Mary's hand was clearly visible.

Paul shoved Mary away from his wife. Mary recovered, and threw her arms around Paul, kissing him passionately.

"Jake, do something," Molly cried.

Jake felt helpless. He pulled Mary away from Paul. "Mary, you're going to have to leave here, before somebody gets hurt," he said.

"No," she shouted. "I ain't leaving here without my Paulie. Oh, Paul, I come a long way to find you, honey. And I ain't leaving here without you."

"I ain't going no where with you," Paul said. "And just look who's talking. Who left who, remember? You're the one that left me for that devilish weasel Henry Gordon. Now, get out of my sight. I don't want nothing else to do with you."

"But I'm your wife, Paul," Mary said. "You can't just throw me out like that."

"No, you're *not* my wife," Paul said. "I got a divorce from you. You're not my wife anymore. Molly's my wife, now. I love her, and we aim to have a life together. Now, get out of here."

"I didn't know nothing about no divorce," Mary said. "Nobody told me about it. Why didn't you tell me?"

"I didn't know where you were, Mary," Paul said. "Besides, I didn't really care where you were, long as you weren't around me."

"I want proof," Mary said. "Where's the divorce papers?" She started to go inside the house.

"You're not going in my house," Molly screamed, as she blocked the door.

Paul pulled Mary back away from the door.

"Mary," he said. "John Campbell's got a copy of the papers. Go talk to him. Now, please leave here."

Jake had heard enough. Suddenly he picked Mary up, and carried her to the buggy.

"You put me down," she said. Mary began beating his back with her hand bag.

Jake managed to hang on till he reached the buggy. He had to throw her into the drivers seat, and is was not a gentle landing for Mary.

"I believe Paul wants you to leave, and that's just what you aim to do," Jake said.

Mary took the whip, and tried to strike Jake. But he took the whip away from her. He handed her the reins, and slapped the horse's flank. The buggy moved forward, then Jake hit the horse with the whip. Mary left at a high rate of speed.

"I'll be back for you, Paul," Mary shouted.

After Mary was safely out of sight, Jake mounted his horse, and followed her.

He'd make sure she went back to town, then he'd tell Big Jim.

Paul embraced his wife, and they went inside their home.

19 THE ORPHANAGE

They'd been hearing about it for over a year. Every wagon train that came through now had experienced Indian attacks This time, several people had been killed, and four children were orphaned.

Big Jim brought the children to James and Carolyn.

"We'll gladly take them," James said. "We've got some empty rooms now. The boy can help me take care of the place."

James wouldn't admit it, but he needed the help. He'd been having some problems lately, and even went to see Dr. Morgan. But still, the pain in his left arm continued. And he had to rest often, now. He just didn't feel good, but was too stubborn to say much about it.

The oldest children, Matthew and Millie were both teenagers. He was fourteen, and already six foot tall. Millie was twelve, 'going on thirteen.' She was as shy as Matthew was talkative.

"I'll swan, that boy can talk your hind leg off," Carolyn said.

"Where did you get a saying like that?" James said.

She laughed. "Oh, that's just something I heard Malindy say a few days ago," she said. "But he's already such a handsome young man."

The two little girls, Emily and Marie were five and two. Marie carried her doll everywhere she went. Neither of them smiled, nor talked very much. But everyone at the boarding house fell in love with them, and helped take care of them.

John did all the paperwork to establish the orphanage, and Martha agreed to give the new children special schooling.

"I want them to smile," she told Carolyn. "If I can just get one smile from them this school term, it'll be worth everything."

Calvin and Malindy had been helping Bobby and Sarah set up the cheese plant. Malindy and several other ladies from the community would be making cheese, butter, buttermilk, sweet milk and cream. Bobby and Sarah had canvassed all the businesses and residents in Oregon City, and nearly all who didn't have a cow had agreed to buy cheese, butter and milk from him. Now they set out to survey the other settlements. The results were very good, even overwhelming at times.

They would be able to open for business on December first. Bobby would bring in the milk supply every morning, and the process would begin.

"Who's going to milk all them cows, Bobby?" Newt Moore said. "With all of the folks at the plant, that don't leave nobody to do the milking. What are you going to do about that? Me and Brown can't do it all by ourselves."

Bobby hadn't even thought about that. He'd been so busy lining up customers that he'd neglected to hire farm hands. Now he only had four days to find enough people to milk one hundred fifty cows.

"And what do you aim to put all that milk in?" Jeremiah Brown said. "All you got is some milk buckets. But it'll take a lot more than a bucket or two for this job."

While Newt stood on the street corner with the job offers, Bobby went to each settlement buying barrels, buckets, and other large containers.

"Well, how'd you do?" Bobby said. "Did we get enough people to milk the cows?"

"I think so," Moore said. "I hired ten people, plus you and Sarah and the kids."

"I doubt if them kids can milk one cow between them," he said. "But it'll have to do, I guess."

Moore and Brown would bring the cows into the barn, and feed them. They'd have everything ready for the milkers to start work at six Monday morning.

Bobby put his collection of buckets and barrels on the wagon. As soon as the milk pail was full, it would be emptied into these containers. When the wagon was full of milk, Bobby would take it to the plant, then return for another wagon load.

"Well, it works on paper, anyway," Moore said. "I guess we're about as ready as we'll ever be."

It rained for two days, then turned sharply colder. James had been fixing the leaky roof over Mr. Williams room. Finally, he got the repair job finished, and came down the ladder. Matthew was waiting for him, and took the ladder to the shed.

"Matthew," James called.

He turned around to see James slump to the ground. Matthew dropped the ladder, and ran to James.

The pain in James's chest was so intense that he couldn't talk, or move. He thought he would surely die with the next breath.

Matthew was frightened. He got up and ran into the kitchen.

"Mrs. Greene," he said. The panic in his voice was evident. "Come quick. It's Mr. Greene. Something's wrong with him. Hurry."

Carolyn and Helen ran to James. The others went to the back door to see what had occurred.

"Matthew, go get Dr. Morgan," Helen said. "Run as fast as you can."

"Oh, dear God, don't let nothing happen to my James," Carolyn prayed. She sat on the ground, and lifted his head into her lap. That seemed to help him breathe better.

Matthew ran as fast as he could. It just wasn't fair. He'd had to watch their parents die, now he'd have to watch James die. By the time he reached Dr. Morgan's office, he was crying so much he could hardly see.

"Dr. Morgan, come quick," Matthew said.

Dr. Morgan looked up from his apothecary table.

"Whoa, son, slow down," Dr. Morgan said. "Now, what's the matter?"

Matthew explained while the doctor got his black bag. They ran back to the boarding house.

"Looks like he's had a heart attack," Dr. Morgan told Carolyn. "He's going to need lots of rest. And he absolutely cannot do any more work around here."

"But what will we do now?" Carolyn said.

"Carolyn, you've got to keep him off his feet, and make him rest. You don't have any choice. He'll die, if he tries to work," Dr. Morgan said.

"Can you help him?"

"I've got some powders here that may help," Dr. Morgan said. "But it's up to The Almighty. Can somebody help me get him to bed?"

"No, I'm not going to bed," James said. "I'm not a bit sleepy. It's the middle of the day. I can't go to bed in the day time."

"James Greene, you old stubborn mule," Dr. Morgan said. "Then we'll lay you down on that sofa in the parlor. But you are going to lay down, James. And you're going to stay there till time to go to bed. Do you understand me?"

"Yeah, I reckon," James said. "But there's a lot of work I need to do here. When can I go back to work?"

"Now, James, you can't work no more," Dr. Morgan said. "From what I can tell, you're lucky to be alive. I don't want you to even carry in the wood. You're just going to have to let somebody else do the work here. What about that Matthew? He seems to be a fine boy. Let him do some of the work."

James reluctantly agreed. But he was also in too much distress to offer any more resistance. Matthew and Dr. Morgan carried him to the sofa, and Carolyn gave him a pillow and a blanket.

"Carolyn, you go be with James," Helen said. "We can finish up here, can't we, girls?"

They all agreed, and shooed her out of the kitchen.

Martha ran all the way from the schoolhouse to the boarding house. She was crying, and praying as she ran.

The parlor door flew open, and Martha ran in.

James had drifted off to sleep, and Carolyn stood to greet her. She told Martha the details.

"We'll have to find somebody to help Matthew," Carolyn said. "He's a good boy, but he don't know how to fix things the way James does."

"I'll see if John can help find someone," Martha said. "Will you be all right?"

"Yes," Carolyn said. "We'll be fine. Go on home, dear. There's lot's of people here who will help us tonight."

Help arrived the next day. Thomas Perkins knocked on the door at eight o'clock sharp.

"Morning, Mrs. Greene," Perkins said. "I'm Thomas Perkins. Jerry and Sally Connelly sent me over. They said you all might need somebody to work here."

Carolyn could have hugged him. *Thank You, Lord. And thank you, Jerry and Sally* she thought. They negotiated an arrangement where Thomas could work for his room and board, and help teach Matthew, too.

It had been a very trying week in Oregon City. Everyone relaxed more as Saturday dawned clear, and cold. They looked forward to being refreshed by the Sunday church service.

The little pot-bellied stove was cherry red, and it felt nice inside the church. Henry and Minnie Thatcher had donated a wagon load of firewood, and Reverend Martin was pleased.

Carolyn was thankful that James was getting better. It was hard to keep him still, and he was very unwilling to lie down. She caught him several times trying to sneak away from the parlor. She came to church this morning grateful to God that he was still with her.

Reverend Martin dismissed his congregation with a note of encouragement.

"Folks, one of our members is down," he said. "James Greene had a heart attack the other day. Go by and see him. He's our friend and neighbor, and the Good Book says to help people in need. And when you pray, you might mention his name. Now, let's be dismissed in a word of prayer…"

"Carolyn, if you need any heavy work done, I'd be right glad to help you," Henry said.

"Thank you, Henry," she said. "I may have to call you sometime."

Martha, John and the children spent Sunday afternoon with Carolyn and James. Martha helped Carolyn, while John attended to James.

Bobby's cheese plant opened as scheduled on Monday morning. The farm workers had half the cows milked, and the milk loaded on the wagon by eight o'clock. Bobby took the first wagon load to town. They stored it in the 'milk house', a separate room from the processing area. The milk house had no heat, so the milk would keep longer. Malindy had organized the routine. She showed them how to make butter in one section. Buttermilk was collected there, and taken to it's room. Cheese was made in another

195

area, and sweet milk and cream was kept in yet a different place. Today's fresh milk for sale was out in the store front. When they were ready, the cheese and other products would be placed in the store front, also.

Bobby came back to his farm for the second load of milk. By the time he got back, the cows had all been milked, and the second milk wagon was full. He delivered the milk, returned with the empty containers, and got everything ready for tomorrow.

Bobby and Sarah were pleased with such a good beginning. The customers seemed happy with all the products. Malindy was satisfied that the workers all knew how to make good butter, cheese, and buttermilk.

"Anybody can churn butter," Malindy said. "But good butter takes a little more time. And they're doing it right. It sure does taste good, too."

Thursday morning, Bobby was taking the second load of milk to town. Just as he came into town, a horse and buggy came out of nowhere, and cut in front of him. He turned the horses sharply to the right to avoid the collision. The load of milk shifted in the wagon, causing the wagon to overturn. The street turned white with his precious cargo, the barrels broke apart, and the wagon was damaged. Bobby and his horses escaped unharmed, but he was very upset.

There was nothing he could do but clean up the mess. Passers by offered their sympathy, but no one offered to help. Finally he had everything picked up. Several cats suddenly appeared, and began drinking the puddles of milk. Bobby wanted to chase them away.

"I hope you drink so much you get sick," he yelled at the cats. "You always want a handout, don't you?"

Big Jim heard the crash, and came by to see what happened.

"You would get here after I got it all picked up," Bobby said.

"Well, old Mrs. Caruthers got in my way," Jim said. "You know how slow the poor old thing is. She can't help it, Bobby. Now, what in the world happened here?"

Bobby told him.

"I'll bet it was Mary Smith," Jim said. "I saw her driving that buggy fast as the horses could go. Did you recognize the driver?"

"Mary Smith? Paul's ex-wife?" Bobby said. "What's she doing here, Jim?"

"Oh, she's just causing trouble, Bobby, just like she used to," Jim said. "Do you think it was her?"

"Well, it could've been," Bobby said. "It was a woman driving the buggy."

"I'll talk to her, if I can catch up with her," Jim said. "I'm looking for an excuse to run her out of here, anyway."

Bobby explained the accident to his workers. He made his deliveries, and tried to think where he could get more barrels. He remembered a place in Portland that he was sure would have barrels.

"Sure, I got barrels," Mr. Meier said. "These are the finest oak barrels this side of Germany. They're made the old fashioned way, and guaranteed not to leak. What kind of still you got?"

"Oh, I don't have a still," Bobby said. "I'm going to haul milk in these."

"Milk? Are you crazy?" Mr. Meier said. "Who ever heard of putting milk in barrels?"

"Well, are you going to sell me some barrels or not?"

"Oh, all right," Meier said. "How many do you want?"

He bought ten new barrels, and returned home.

20 RECOVERY

James continued to make a good recovery. He still didn't feel good, and it was as hard as ever to keep him still. He wandered around the house, pointing out work that needed to be done, giving instructions to Thomas and Matthew. He was underfoot in the kitchen, as well.

"Carolyn, what are we going to do with him?" Susan said. "We all love him to pieces, but we can't even work with him in our way."

"I know," Carolyn said. "I'll try to talk to him. Maybe I'd better talk to Dr. Morgan, too."

Arthur Kelly showed John three different newspapers. They all carried much the same story.

"John, something's wrong," Arthur said. "There's trouble in the southern states. They're actually talking about seceding from the Union."

John read the articles.

"Where did you get these, Arthur?"

"My editor sent them to me," he said. "He'll probably reassign me, somewhere down south."

"According to these articles, many people would even be willing to go to war over the slavery issue," John said. "Do you think there'll be a war?"

"I don't know, John," he said. "But I do know feelings run high about this in Boston, and elsewhere in New England."

"How ironic," John said. "Here we are doing the preliminary work for statehood, while they're talking about leaving the Union. I don't know much about any of the southern states, but I'd sure hate to see this happen."

"So would I," he said. "And I don't know how it would affect things here. There's just no way to tell."

"Well, President Polk wants good settlements out here," John said. "We've got to keep this area together, and drive out the British. If we don't, they'll be back. Then they'll take everything from Alaska to California, and they'll probably go on to the South Pacific."

"Yes," Arthur said. "They'd love to run us out of our own country."

John went back to his office with these thoughts weighing heavily on his mind.

"Hello, Mary," John said. "I heard you were in town. What can I do for you?"

"John, is it true Paul got a divorce from me?" Mary said.

"Yes, he did."

"I want to see the papers."

"All right, Mary," John said. "It'll take a minute to find them. Make yourself comfortable."

She sat quietly.

"Here we are, Mary," John said.

The truth sank in. She never thought Paul would divorce her. She'd always played on his sympathy and love, and now that weapon had been taken away. Well, she'd just have to find a new angle, now.

"Do you need to see a copy of the marriage license?" John said.

"No," Mary said. "No, that won't be necessary. Do I owe you anything?"

"No. I haven't really done anything. These are public records, and there's never a charge."

"Thank you, John," she said. "I must be going. It's good to see you again. Tell Martha hello."

Mary was stunned. Her confidence was shaken, and she didn't notice Big Jim standing before her.

"Good morning, Mary," Jim said.

"Good morning," she mumbled.

"Say, Mary, where was you going the other morning, when you cut in front of Bobby Parker's milk wagon?"

"What?" she said. "What are you talking about?"

"Thursday morning, when you got in that buggy and drove through town like a bat out of Perdition," Jim said. "Where was you going in such a hurry?"

"Oh, I don't know," she said. "I…I don't even remember anything about it."

"Well, I think you owe Bobby for spilling his milk," Jim said. "You could at least offer to pay him for it."

"Pay him for spilled milk? I'll do no such thing, Jim Cross," she said. "And you can't make me, either."

"Yes, I can make you pay him," Jim said. "Under the Provisional Government Law, I can make you pay him. Let's go over there and get this settled right now."

He gripped her arm firmly, and she had to run to keep up with him.

"Bobby, you remember Mary Smith, don't you?" Big Jim said.

"I sure do," Bobby said.

"Is she the woman you saw driving the buggy Thursday morning?"

Bobby looked at her for a moment.

"Yes, sir," he said. "This is who I saw driving that buggy."

"Well, I didn't see you," Mary said.

"Mary, you caused an accident," Jim said.

"I didn't know anything about an accident," she said.

"Bobby, about how much do you figure all that milk was worth?" Jim said.

"Well, I'd say about fifty dollars," Bobby said. "And I spent close to another fifty on new barrels. So, I'd say a hundred dollars ought to do it."

"Now, wait a minute," Mary said. "I ain't paying you that kind of money."

"Bobby, do you want me to arrest her?" Jim said.

"Yeah. If she don't pay for the milk, arrest her," Bobby said.

"Oh, all right," Mary said. She took out a handful of money, and peeled off one hundred dollars. She counted it out to Bobby.

"This is blackmail," she said.

"Now, you be a little more careful when you take your buggy through town, Mary," Jim said. "If you cause anymore trouble, of any kind, I'll force you to leave Oregon City."

"You big bully," she said. "I live here. You can't run me off."

"And I'm the Sheriff here," Jim said. "If I catch you doing anything else, like fighting with Paul or Molly, I'll run you out of here. Now, go on about your business, before you make me plumb mad."

Mary left in a huff.

A few days later, Mr. Peterson arrived to help John. He spoke to Big Jim, as they passed on the street.

"Oh, Jim," he said. "Can I talk to you a minute?"

"Sure. What's on your mind?"

"There's a fellow up around Portland that's been asking about you. Older gentleman, says he's from St. Louis, and come out here on the wagon train with you. Name's Gordon. Do you know him?"

"Uh, oh," Jim said. Big Jim could feel his anger rising. "That's Henry Gordon. But we don't need the likes of him in Portland, or anywhere else." Jim explained Gordon's 'business', his connection to Mary Smith, and Mary's problems in Oregon City.

"I'm sure glad you told me, Jim," Mr. Peterson said. "From the way he acted, I thought there was something wrong. Do you think we should arrest him?"

"Not unless he does something," Jim said. "Just run him out of town. Tell him to go back to St. Louis. I'm fixing to run Mary out, too."

"But they'll just go set up their cathouse somewhere else," Mr. Peterson said.

"Yeah, but at least it won't be here," Jim said.

Later that day, when Mary saw Paul and Molly entering the General Merchandise Store, she became enraged.

When they came out, Paul helped Molly into the wagon, and began loading the supplies.

"Paul, Paul," Mary said. She ran across the street, waving to him.

Molly took the whip out, and lashed Mary across the chest and neck. Mary screamed. Paul wrestled the whip away from Molly, and threw it in the back of the wagon.

"Mary, get out of here," he said.

People watched from doorways, including John and Mr. Peterson. Big Jim came to see what the problem was.

"Jim, arrest that woman," Mary said. "She hit me with that whip. Just look here what she done." The whelp stood out like a big red snake.

"Well, what did you do to them, Mary?"

"I didn't do nothing to them," she said. "I just wanted to talk to my Paulie."

"He ain't your 'Paulie' anymore," Molly said. "And you best be keeping your dirty little hands off of him, too."

"All right, Mary," Jim said. "What'd I tell you this morning? You've got two hours to get your things together, and get out of town."

"I ain't leaving here without my Paulie," Mary said.

"Yes, you will, too," Jim said.

"Mary, I done told you I ain't going no where with you," Paul said. "I put up with you for ten years, and you done things like this all the time." Paul was very angry. He stood up in the wagon bed, shaking with rage, afraid he'd lose all self control.

"Mary, you hurt me time after time," Paul said. "When you left me for Henry Gordon, I swore I'd never take anything from you again. I don't love you no more. I don't want to ever see you again, or ever have anything to do with you. I don't want to harm you, Mary, but if you don't leave me alone, I just might. You'll make me so mad, I won't know what I'm doing."

Mary couldn't believe this. She'd never heard him talk in such a manner, and never thought his temper was dangerous. Mary had never been afraid of him. But she knew he meant every word he'd said.

"Mary, you'd better leave," Big Jim said gently. "Get your things, and leave town. Go back up to Portland, where Henry Gordon's at. And just keep going. Don't come anywhere near this settlement ever again. Do you want me to take you back to the boarding house?"

"No, thank you," she said, very somber. "I'll be gone quick as I can." She turned and left.

"Good-bye, Paul," Mary said, over her shoulder.

"Paul, take me home," Molly said.

Paul stood still, and fought to restrain himself. He knew he'd come very close to tragedy, and it scared him. Paul realized if Mary hadn't left when she did, he fully intended to kill her. That thought made him physically sick, and he lost everything he'd eaten today. When he recovered, he knew it was time to go.

"Let's go home," Paul said. He sat down on the seat beside Molly, and left.

Mary collected her things, and threw them in the buggy. She headed north, toward Portland.

A few days later, Willie came into town, looking for Big Jim.

"I need more horses, Jim," he said. "There's a new settlement going up down south of here, across the mountains. If I can get my stage coaches in there, I can beat that guy in Portland. And you'll never guess who I seen down there."

"Oh?" Jim said. "Who'd you see?" He wasn't at all sure he wanted to know.

"I seen that Mary Smith and Henry Gordon," Willie said. "They'd set up their trade from the saloon. How many men and boys'll end up like Johnny? Jim, it made me so mad, I wanted to go in there and beat the devil out of all of them."

"I know how you feel, Willie," Jim said. He told Willie about Mary's escapades in Oregon City.

"Is Paul and Jake still here?" Willie said. "I've got to get more horses."

Willie visited all afternoon, and spent the night with his parents. The next day, he went to see Paul and Jake.

21 MARTHA'S STUDENTS

It seemed impossible for Martha to convince Millie that she needed to attend school. Millie thought of herself as a grown woman now, capable of conducting her own affairs. Millie thought since Matthew didn't have to attend school, she didn't either. The usual methods of encouragement were just not working.

"What are we going to do, Carolyn?" Martha said. "This child needs to be in school. She can't even count past ten, and she can't read. Matthew is very good with his numbers. He reads well, and knows some history and geography. Emily seems to like school. But I can't get her or Marie to talk very much, and they still don't smile."

"I've never seen you so discouraged," Carolyn said. "I know Millie needs more schooling, but we can't make her go. She just won't listen to us."

"I know," Martha said. "And yes, I've worried about this for weeks, now."

"Let's give it some time, dear," Carolyn said. "Add a little prayer, too."

Martha smiled, and hugged her. She hugged James, and left for home.

Martha's mind was racing ahead, trying to find a way to reach her students.

"You seem distracted tonight," John said. "What's wrong?"

"Oh, nothing," she said. She wasn't ready to ask for help yet.

"Now, don't 'oh, nothing,' me," he said. "You've been like this for days on end. Now, tell me what's wrong."

Martha had to admit her problem. They discussed the situation from every angle they could find. But John didn't have an answer, either. Martha sat up for an hour after everyone else was asleep. Finally she exhausted her nervous energy, and went to bed.

Martha awoke suddenly, and sat up in bed.

"That's it," she said. "That's it. Of course, this'll work. Why didn't I think of it before?"

"Martha, what's the matter with you?" John said. He looked at his pocket watch. The moonlight shined through the cracks enough that he could see the time. "Martha, it's three o'clock in the morning. What are you doing?"

She got up, and began to dress.

"John, I know how to help those children," she said.

"Can't it wait til morning?"

"I suppose *it* could, but I can't," she said. "Go back to sleep. I'll be fine."

He was already asleep.

Martha put more wood in the fireplace, and lit the lamp. She got out her paper, and began writing. She finished her plans just as John was getting up. Now it was time to start breakfast, but she was happy, and excited.

"Will you please explain this to me?" John said.

"I don't think so," she said. "You'll find out when it starts working."

Paul and Jake left to find more horses. This was becoming a good business venture for them. In addition to supplying horses for Willie's stage line, they'd sold to Patrick and Ian's freight company, Bobby's cheese plant, and several farmers.

Big Jim recognized her buggy as she drove through town. He mounted his horse, and followed her from a distance.

I figured that's what she'd do Jim thought. Mary Smith headed for Paul's cabin. *She's trying to catch Paul gone, and pick a fight with Molly. Well, not if I can help it.*

Molly was hanging clothes on the line when Mary drove up. Already with child, she could only wash a few things at a time.

"What do you want?" Molly said.

"Where's Paul?"

"I don't think that's any of your business, Mary," she said. "And I think you ought to leave while you still can." She hung another shirt on the line.

"Well, I've still got something to say to him," Mary said. "But since he ain't man enough to come out here and face me, I'll just say it to you."

"You'll do no such thing," Molly said. She pulled the pistol out of her apron pocket. "Now, you get back in that buggy, and get off this property real fast like. And don't you ever come around me or Paul again. Do you hear me?"

"Now, Molly," Mary said. She was a little scared. Paul scared her the last time she saw him, and now, this.

"You wouldn't shoot me, would you, Molly," she said. "I ain't got no gun. I come here peaceable."

Big Jim stopped at the crest of the ridge. He could see them facing each other, and knew they were arguing, but was too far away to hear them. He ran toward them.

"Get off our land, Mary," she said. "So help me, I'll shoot, if you don't leave."

Mary stood her ground.

Molly cocked the hammer, took aim at Mary's feet, and fired. Mary screamed. She wasn't hurt, just terrified.

Molly's hands were shaking, as she cocked the hammer again, and took aim.

"This time, the bullet won't hit the dirt, Mary," she said. "This time, it'll hit you. Now, leave here, while you can."

"Molly, I ain't done you no harm," Mary said. "But I'm going to tell Big Jim that you tried to kill me."

"What is it you want to tell me, Mary?" Big Jim said.

Mary screamed again. She was nervous and jumpy.

"Molly, are you all right?" Jim said.

"I'm fine, Jim," she said. "But I'm getting sick." She walked to the nearby tree, and threw up.

"Mary, you're under arrest for disturbing the peace," Jim said.

"What? I didn't do nothing to that woman. I just come out here to talk to Paul, and she attacked me."

Jim drew his gun.

"Mary, you hold still while I tie your hands," Jim said. "Now, you get in that buggy."

"Well, you've got my hands tied behind my back. How do you think I can get in the buggy?"

"Just like this," Jim said. He picked her up and sat her in the back of the buggy. "You're going to spend a couple of nights in jail."

Big Jim started toward Molly. He thought of something, and went back to the buggy.

"I don't want you to leave here til I'm ready," he said. Then he tied her feet together.

Mary was furious. "Jim Cross, you let me go," she screamed. "You can't do this to me. I ain't done nothing. Come back here, and let me loose." She kicked and cursed.

Jim walked over to Molly.

"I'm all right," she said. "Thank you, Jim."

"Did she hurt you?"

"No," Molly said. "But Jim, I sure come close to hurting her. Am I in trouble?"

"No," Jim said. "You're not in trouble. Do you need anything till Paul gets back?"

211

"No," she said. "We're…I'm fine. Paul took care of everything before they left. He'll be home in a few days. But thank you, Jim."

"If you need anything, you let me know," Jim said. He tipped his hat to her, and turned toward the problem of Mary Smith.

Jim tied his horse to the back of the buggy, and transported Mary to the Oregon City jail.

Martha couldn't wait for school to be out today. She had a mission to accomplish, and was anxious to get started.

"Johnny, Johnny," Martha called to his taxi wagon.

"Hi, Martha," Johnny said. "Where you want to go?"

"I need to go see either Jenny and Charles, or Becky and Billy Joe," she said. "Can you get me there and back before dark?"

"Yep, I think I can," Johnny said.

They chatted constantly, and laughed at all the funny things from their common adventures on the wagon train. Martha couldn't help but notice how many times Johnny took out the flask of whiskey. She knew his injuries must be painful, but wished he could find another method of relief. Yet, what else was there?

The taxi wagon pulled up in Becky's yard. Smoke rolled out the chimney, and something smelled good.

"Want me to wait for you?" Johnny said.

"Yes," Martha said.

Johnny got down, and helped Martha out of the wagon. She stared at him. But his right arm was very strong, and he lifted her with ease. She couldn't stand to see him limp. Martha wondered if perhaps she should help him in and out of the wagon, but knew she must not do that. Johnny knocked on the door with the tip of his cane.

"Well, hi Martha, Johnny," Becky said. "Come on in. I was just starting supper. Can you stay?"

"No, thank you, dear," Martha said. "We just have a minute or two."

"Yeah. I'll stay, if you'll feed me," Johnny said.

Becky laughed, and told him there were some biscuits left over from breakfast.

"Becky, I'll get to the point," Martha said. "I need you and Jenny to help me. Will you do that?"

"Why, sure, Martha," she said. "You know we'd all do anything in the world for you. I would, and I know Jenny would, too."

"First, I need to know something," Martha said. "How's your studies going? Are you having any problems?"

"Well, a few," Becky said. "I'm still not good with the Latin. I don't know if I can ever do it, Martha."

"How's your French? Do you need my help with that?"

"Well, yes, I sure do," Becky said. "And I don't understand some of this arithmetic, either."

"Good," Martha said. "I mean, it's good that you realize you need help. I'll be glad to help you. Can you come by Carolyn's Boarding House, let's say on Saturday afternoon?"

"Yeah, I guess so," she said. "Martha, what's this all about?"

Martha laughed, and explained about her problem students.

"So, I thought if you and Jenny would let them see me helping you, maybe they'd get more enthused about school," Martha said.

"Well, I think that's a good idea," Becky said. "We'll be glad to come. Besides, that way, we can stay with the folks till Sunday evening."

"Then it's settled," Martha said. She stood to leave, and bid farewell to Becky. Johnny grabbed an extra biscuit, gently pulled his sister's hair, and headed for the wagon.

Jenny was also preparing supper. Charles was chopping wood when they arrived.

"Hi, Martha," he said. "What brings you up here? Come on in. Jenny'll be right glad to see you."

While Johnny and Charles brought in the wood, and milked the cow, Martha repeated her plan to Jenny.

"Millie thinks she's a grown woman, and doesn't need to learn anything," Martha said. "I want her to see just how necessary it really is for adults to continue learning."

"I sure need help," Jenny said. "Martha, I don't like this philosophy class. And I don't agree with any of it, either."

"Just bring your books, and I'll help you" Martha said.

Charles was still his obstinate self.

"But Martha, if that girl don't want to go to school, why make her do it?" he said. "It'll just get her hopes up for nothing."

"Now, Charles," Jenny said. "You don't have no say-so here. This ain't me we're talking about. At least I could read, and do my numbers. And so could you. But she can't. And I believe she needs at least that much, don't you?"

Charles had to admit that everyone needed some education. He finally gave in, and agreed to be at Carolyn's on Saturday afternoon.

Martha and Johnny headed home.

"Where in the world have you been?" John said. "It's after dark, and I was worried about you."

Martha kissed him, and began explaining her plan.

"You know, that just might work," John said. "It'll sure be interesting, won't it?"

"Are you still mad at me?"

John laughed. "No, I guess not," he said. "Now, when can we eat?"

"As soon as I get it ready," she said.

Carolyn and James knew they needed to add more rooms to their boarding house.

"But I just don't think I can do it," James said. "I sure hate to admit it, but Dr. Morgan's right. I can't work any more. We'll have to hire somebody to do it."

"What about Henry Thatcher?" Carolyn said. "He offered to help us a few weeks ago, right after you got sick."

"All right, that's what we'll do," James said. "I know he'll do a mighty good job. Let's get word to him tomorrow."

"Do you think we ought to buy some land, get a cow, and some chickens?" Carolyn said.

"Let me think about that," he said.

22 THE PLAN

John entered the Provisional Government Office with a lot of things on his mind. Big Jim was already there, explaining about Mary Smith.

"Jim, I'll ride with you down to the new settlement," Mr. Peterson said. "We'll see what kind of law they've got. Maybe they can keep Mary away from here."

"I sure would appreciate that," Jim said. "Can you go tomorrow? I'd like to get rid of this problem as fast as I can."

"Sure," Peterson said. "Now, John, let's get to work on some of these things we talked about the other day."

Martha had been thinking of Grandma Catherine lately. *By now, she would've had all those kids anxious for school every day* Martha thought. *I sure wish there was a way I could talk to her when I need her. Guess we'll just have to go back and visit her.*

Everyday, Martha would tell Millie and Emily about her 'other students'.

"All right, Mrs. Campbell," Millie said. "Just who are these 'other students?' I don't see nobody else around here."

"Oh, you'll meet them Saturday," Martha said. "They need my help with some of their studies."

"I'll believe it when I see it," Millie said.

Millie was the perfect housekeeper. She took it upon herself to sweep the floors, dust the furniture, make the beds, and help with the laundry. Matthew took care of the maintenance problems, while Thomas and Henry built two extra rooms. Of course, James couldn't keep from 'assisting' Matthew. And more often than not, Matthew needed his help. Carolyn had to admit she really needed Millie's help.

Emily and Marie kept to themselves, seldom talked, and never smiled. They were eating good now, and had gained a few pounds. Millie helped them with bath time, and bedtime, but the girls wouldn't play with the other children.

"Well, I see why Martha is so upset about these children," Susan said. "It breaks my heart to see them like this. How can we get them out of their shell?" No one could answer that question.

"My, you look happy and lovely today," John said. "Any special reason?"

"Yes," Martha said. "Today's Saturday."

"Huh?"

217

"Today I hope we can help Millie realize how much she needs school," Martha said. "I just know this will make a difference."

John kissed her, as she poured his coffee.

"I really believe it will help her," he said. "How long will you be gone today?"

"Probably all afternoon," Martha said. She kissed him good-bye, and hugged the children. She climbed on board the buggy, and headed for Carolyn's Boarding House.

Becky and Billy Joe arrived first. She hadn't felt good all morning, and the wagon ride seemed to make things worse. But she gathered her courage, and prepared for lessons in Latin.

"Millie, I want you to meet someone," Martha said.

Millie stared at Becky.

"This is Becky, and her husband, Billy Joe," Martha said. "Becky is one of my best students. She attends the Oregon Institute. And I'm very proud of her."

"Hi, Millie," Becky said, and Billy Joe waved to her.

"Hi," Millie said. Then she turned to Martha.

"I thought you said they was students," Millie said. "She's a woman, and in a family way, too. Where's the kids at?"

"I'm a student, Millie," Becky said. "I go to the Oregon Institute over near Salem. Martha's been helping me with my studies."

"You still go to school?" Millie said. "How many times did teacher hold you back?"

"Millie, the Oregon Institute is a college," Martha said. "That's where you learn a lot more things than at the school here in Oregon City."

"Why do you keep on going to school?" Millie said.

"Cause I want to learn a lot of different things, Millie," Becky said. "Sometimes I don't understand them, and that's when I need Martha's help. But it's wonderful to learn new things, Millie."

A few minutes later, Jenny and Charles arrived. He was still fussing.

"Charles, you'll not tell that child no such thing," Jenny said.

Martha introduced Jenny as her other student, while Charles went to the kitchen in search of something good.

They had decided previously to just let Millie wander in and out at will. If she got curious, they'd seize the opportunity.

After the noon meal, the girls and Martha got down to business. James, Billy Joe and Charles went out to supervise the new construction.

Their studies did attract a crowd. Emily and Marie came in and sat beside Jenny.

"Jenny, this is Emily, and her sister, Marie," Martha said.

Jenny smiled at both of them, and sat Marie in her lap. Emily sat very close to her side.

Martha guided Jenny through the chapter of Philosophy that had caused her so much trouble.

"Now, I know you don't agree with this," Martha said. "But do you see what he's trying to say?"

"Yes," Jenny said. "Now that you've explained why he feels that way, what he's saying makes sense. But I still don't agree."

219

"Honey, you don't have to agree with him," Martha said. "Always remember that. In this class, just look at things from other points of view, and you'll be fine. Now, you start the writing assignment for this chapter, and I'll help Becky with the Latin."

Jenny began writing, while Emily and Marie watched intently.

Millie came in with the other children. They got water, and sugar cookies. Millie stopped to see what was going on.

Jenny paused to think for a moment.

"Whatcha doing?" Millie said.

"Shhh," Emily said. "She's thinking."

Martha's heart leaped for joy. Jenny and Becky were smiling, and they looked at Martha. There were tears in Martha's eyes, and a big smile on her face.

"She's writing down what she thinks about things in this book," Martha said.

"What's the book about?" Millie said.

"Well, this chapter is about a man named Voltaire, and what he thought about a lot of things," Martha said.

"You said you don't agree with him," Millie said. "If you don't like him, why do you care what he thinks?"

Martha didn't know whether to cry with joy, or laugh with joy.

"Well, to tell the truth, I don't like him at all, either," Martha said. "But it makes things more interesting to know what other people think."

Millie was hooked. For the next hour, her questions were endless. Martha, Jenny and Becky patiently answered her queries, and Carolyn baked more cookies.

"Oh, let's take a break," Martha said.

Emily and Marie stayed close to Jenny, while Millie went back out to play. Charles and Billy Joe came back, and joined the girls on the sofa. Charles put his arm around Jenny, and Marie climbed in his lap. She snuggled down with her doll, and went to sleep.

Charles was amazed, and Jenny loved it. Martha was filled with joy. Becky and Billy Joe couldn't believe what they saw. All in all, it was a wonderful afternoon.

Jenny finished her writing assignment, while Becky and Martha focused on Latin.

Charles was captivated by two little girls. He told them stories, and played games with them. He took them outside to play with the others, and helped them learn Red Rover. When the game was over, they all came back inside. He carried Marie on his shoulders, while Emily held his hand. The children ran to the kitchen, and Emily had Charles in tow. He served them more cookies and milk.

Martha and Becky looked up from her studies to see this wonderful event, and have coffee with Carolyn.

"I never dreamed all this would happen," Martha said. "I just thought it would be good for Millie, and it is. But this is a miracle."

"God works in mysterious ways," Carolyn said. "We've all tried to reach these children since the day they got here. Charles and Jenny have done the impossible."

"I…I don't know what to say," Jenny said. "Look at him. He's absolutely happy. We've talked about starting our family. Then we decided to wait till I get through school. That is, if I ever get through."

"Of course, you'll get through," Martha said. "In fact, you'll both graduate with honors."

"I don't know, Martha," Becky said. "This is the hardest thing I've ever done in my life."

"Now, listen here, both of you," Martha said. "No student of mine ever fails to graduate. Both of you are going to graduate, right on time, with the rest of your class. Now, let's get back to work."

Millie came and sat beside Becky. She watched as Becky struggled with Latin phrases.

Finally, curiosity got the best of her.

"I can't make heads or tails out of that stuff," she said. "It just looks like a bunch of hen scratches to me."

Martha explained the Latin words, and why Becky was taking this course. This seemed to satisfy her for a moment, and she went back outside with the other children.

A few minutes later, Millie was back at Becky's side. This time, Becky was working a math problem. Millie watched eagerly, but without comment. She returned to the kitchen.

"Mrs. Greene, you all swept the floors, and done the cleaning and laundry before me and Matthew come here, didn't you?" Millie said.

"Why, yes, we did, honey," Carolyn said.

"So, you all could do it again, if you had to. Couldn't you?"

"Why, sure," Carolyn said. "We've done things like that all our lives." She knew this had to be leading somewhere, but wanted Millie to say it herself.

Millie took a couple of cookies, and went back to Becky and Martha.

"Mrs. Campbell, can I ask you a question?" Millie said.

"Of course, Millie," Martha said. "What is it?"

"If I come to your school Monday morning, you won't make me read that there Latin, will you? That stuff don't make a bit of sense to me."

Martha could've danced a jig. Becky and Jenny smiled, and Carolyn shared their joy.

"No, Millie, you don't have to learn Latin," Martha said. "And if there's anything you don't understand, I'll be glad to help you."

"Just like you're helping Becky and Jenny?"

"Just like I'm helping them now," Martha said. "Now, go play with the others."

After she went outside, the parlor erupted in squeals of delight. They laughed and cried with joy.

"This is wonderful," Martha said.

"Thank the Good Lord," Carolyn said. "We need to celebrate. I'll go bake us a cake."

When the lessons were finished, and the cake consumed, Martha headed home. She was ecstatic, and couldn't wait to tell John

John was milking the cows when she got home. She raced the buggy up to the barn, and leaped off the seat. Martha ran in the barn.

"John, John," she said. "We did it! It worked. Millie will be at school Monday morning."

The cow was startled, and switched her tail in Martha's direction, then stomped her foot.

"Martha, calm down," John said. "You're going to scare this poor thing half to death. She'll kick me, if you do much more."

"John, this has been the most amazing day of my life," she said. Martha grabbed him, pulled him up from the milk stool, and kissed him passionately.

John held her for a long moment, sharing her gladness.

"I'm proud of you, honey," he said. "I knew you could do this."

"But it really wasn't me," she said. "It was actually Becky and Jenny, and their desire to learn that did it. And Charles and Jenny. Honey, you won't believe this."

He sat back down, and began milking again. Martha told him the details. He looked up and smiled.

"You know, you haven't even hugged your own kids yet," John said. "I've built a little play pen for Carolyn in the hay, and Johnny's gathering the eggs. Go say hi to them, while I finish milking."

"I'm sorry," Martha said. "I'm just so happy tonight that I forgot about everything else." Martha went to her daughter, but Carolyn was asleep. It brought to mind images of another Babe asleep in the hay on a cold winter night long ago. Martha knelt by her daughters play pen, and thanked Him for all her blessings.

Becky and Billy Joe went to see Calvin and Malindy, while Charles and Jenny stayed at the boarding house. Emily and Marie never let Charles out of their sight. But he loved it, and entertained them all evening. Jenny and Charles tucked them in bed. Marie held onto Charles.

"It's ok, honey," Charles said. "We'll see you in the morning." He kissed her forehead, and gently laid her back in bed.

"Jenny, wake up," Charles said. "Is that somebody knocking on our door?"

"What?" Jenny said. "I don't hear anything."

"Listen," he said.

The knock came again. It was a very soft, and they thought they'd imagined it. Then the knock came a little louder. Charles got up, and opened the door. There stood Emily and Marie.

"Girls, what's the matter?" Jenny said.

"We're scared," Emily said. Marie nodded in agreement, and clutched her doll.

Charles turned, and looked at Jenny. They both grinned with happiness.

"Come on to bed, girls," Charles said.

The girls snuggled in between them, and went to sleep.

23 WHOLE HOG, OR NOTHIN'

"**B**ecky, you all hurry up," Johnny said. He'd waited half an hour, and was getting annoyed. "I ain't going to take the blame for you being late to class."

"We'll be ready in a minute," Becky said.

"Well, you'd better june around," he said. "I got some more people to take to Salem, so you better come on. I want to be back home at a decent hour."

Finally, Becky and Billy Joe climbed in the stagecoach. Billy Joe tried to pay Johnny, but he refused.

"You're family," Johnny said. "I never charge my family."

Jenny and Charles found it difficult to leave the girls.

"Can we come with you?" Emily said.

"Not this time, honey," Jenny said. "Maybe we can come back next weekend, and visit some more."

Marie wouldn't let go of Charles. One little arm was around his neck, while the other arm held her doll.

"We have to go," he said. "I'll bring you and Emily some apples next week. Would you like to have some apples?"

Marie nodded her head, and smiled at him. He kissed her forehead, and she released her arm from his neck. They hugged the girls, and left for Salem.

"Charles, what are we going to do about these girls?" Jenny said.

He shook his head. "I don't know. I never thought anything like that would happen. And we better think long and hard about this."

"I know it," she said. "Part of me wants to keep them, maybe even adopt them. And part of me knows we can't. We don't have a thing to offer them."

"That's just exactly how I feel," Charles said. "Maybe we should talk to our folks."

Martha walked into her classroom, and said good morning to the children.

"Children, I want you to welcome our newest student, Millie Kirkland. She'll be in our sixth grade," Martha said. She assigned Millie a seat behind Jimmy Willis. He turned around and grinned at her. They settled into class, and Martha answered all Millie's question.

At recess, Jimmy pulled Millie's hair. She chased him down. He pulled her hair again. Millie slapped him, knocking him down. In an instant, other kids swarmed around them. Jimmy scrambled up, as the older boys taunted him.

"What's the matter, Jimmy?" Billy said. "Did *she* knock you down?"

Martha heard the commotion, and came out to see what had happened.

"All right, children," Martha said. "What started this?"

"He pulled my hair," Millie said.

"Jimmy, did you pull her hair?"

"Well, uh,…"

"Did you pull her hair? Tell me the truth, Jimmy."

"Yeah, I guess so," he said.

"Millie, did you hit him?"

"Yes, 'um," Millie said.

"The rest of you children go back inside," Martha said.

As the others left for the class, Martha took Millie and Jimmy by their arms, and marched them to the opposite corners of the room.

"Now, you two will stay in the corner for one hour. When school is out, I'll take you home myself. Jimmy, I want to talk to your parents. Then I'll talk to Millie. Do you understand?"

"Yes, Ma'am," Jimmy said. Millie nodded.

The class begin to laugh.

"That's enough," Martha snapped. "All of you, write in your tablets 'I will not laugh' two hundred times. Now get busy."

Martha slammed her book on the desk. She was frustrated. She'd been so happy for Millie to be in class, and now, some disappointment. Finally, she calmed down, and resumed class.

Jenny and Charles pondered their problem all week. Emotionally, they were pulled in two very different directions.

"It just about broke my heart to leave them," Charles said. "I never thought I could feel that way about children. I always thought if I felt that way, they'd be *my* children. But look at us, honey. We ain't got nothing, we just barely get by. I don't see how we could raise two little girls."

"And what about relatives of these children?" Jenny said. "It would just kill me to bring them home, take care of them and love them. Then in a year or two, some long, lost uncle shows up to take them away from us. I don't think I could stand that, Charles."

"Well, one thing about it. If I take care of them, ain't nobody going to take them away from me," Charles said. "If we decide to do this, we'll adopt them."

"Charles, I don't have any classes tomorrow," Jenny said. "Let's go talk to our folks. I want to know what Momma and Daddy think about this."

"Yeah," he said. "I reckon that's a good idea."

Malindy and Calvin had heard about the two little girls. As Jenny and Charles explained the situation to them, Malindy realized there was only one solution.

"Well, I don't see what your problem is," Malindy said. "Do you love them kids, or not?"

"Well, yeah, I reckon I do love them," Charles said.

"I do, too, Momma," Jenny said.

"Honey, a family ain't built on money. It's built on love," Malindy said. "Me and Pa raised all you kids, didn't we?"

Jenny nodded.

"We never did have any money," Malindy said. "The most we ever had was when we sold the farm to get enough money to get on that wagon train. And we ain't had no money to speak of since then. But that never stopped us from loving you kids, and taking good care of you. Them's mighty sweet little babies, Jenny. And if you and Charles love them, then give them a home."

Jenny and Charles broke into smiles and laughter.

"I guess I needed to hear you tell me what I wanted so bad," Jenny said.

"Now, Charles," Calvin said. "If you take them kids, remember, it's whole hog, or nothin'. You go talk to John. Adopt them kids, and make it legal. That way, nobody can take them away from you."

Supper never tasted so good to Charles and Jenny. They were happy and excited.

"I want to talk to my Pa," Charles said. They got in the wagon for the bumpy ride to his parents.

Charles was somewhat surprised to hear them echo Calvin's sentiment.

"Boy, you better adopt them girls," Pa said. "Only thing about it son, you ain't got no money. I don't see how on earth you can manage this."

"Well, Pa," Charles said. "A wise little woman told me a while ago that a family ain't built on money, it's built on love. And I think I've got plenty of love."

"Yeah, I think you do, too, son."

They drove back to Salem happy and content, making plans for their new family.

On Sunday afternoon, Becky and Billy Joe, Jenny and Charles gathered around the family table. Malindy had outdone herself with this meal. Most of her children were there, and she enjoyed every minute of this.

After dinner, Jenny and Charles went to see "their girls," and Charles brought the apples he'd promised them.

Becky needed Martha's advice.

"Martha, I'm awful tired of being the only woman in my classes," she said. "I'm sick and tired of those stupid men making fun of me, making dirty jokes cause I'm in a family way. How can I learn anything, with them acting like that? Even one or two of my professors have done that."

"Now, listen here," Martha said. "You're not going to give up. Do you hear me?"

"But, Martha…"

"Becky, you're not about to quit. If they make fun of you, you show them that you're a good student. You study twice as hard, and make better grades than they get. It's time for you to prove that a woman like you belongs in the same school with the men. They can make it hard on you, but don't you back down an inch. You stay in class, and keep your grades up. I'll help you all I can."

Becky cried. She calmed her emotions, and continued. "I've wanted more education for a long time. Now, I've got my chance, only they make fun of me. It's getting awful hard to walk in the classroom."

"Becky, there's some things we just have to rise above," Martha said. "I guess this is one of those things. Don't stoop to their level. You've got a good, sound mind. Use it. Beat them at their own game. What classes are the hardest?"

Becky told her that French class was difficult. "Even this professor thinks I can't learn it because I'm a woman," she said.

"That's easy to mend," Martha said. "We'll study French a lot more." Before the afternoon was over, Becky's French was much improved.

"Becky, go all out on your studies."

Becky nodded, and turned her attention back to the French lessons.

Jenny and Charles greeted the girls with hugs and apples. Jenny took Emily, and Charles had Marie.

"You should have seen those kids after you left the other day," Carolyn said. "They cried and cried. They really missed you."

"Well, Carolyn," Charles said. "I think we can solve that problem. We're going to take them home with us."

"We're going to talk to John, and adopt them," Jenny said.

Carolyn was thrilled. "Why, I think that's wonderful," she said.

"Girls, would you like to go home with us?" Charles said.

"Can we stay forever?" Emily said.

"Of course, you can," Jenny said. "We love you and Marie. And we want to be your new Mommie and Daddy. Would you like that?"

"Yes," Emily said. Marie nodded, and smiled at Charles.

They talked a while, and the girls finished their apples.

"Girls, let's go talk to John," Charles said. "Then we'll come back, and get your things, and you can go home with us."

Even Marie laughed and giggled with delight. Charles carried her on his shoulders out to the wagon.

Willie stopped by for a visit, as Charles and Jenny were leaving.

"Yeah, I heard about you and the girls," he said. "Things'll be just fine," he said, as he shook Charles's hand. "Me and Betty Sue's got one on the way, now. Your kids can help take care of my kid."

Willie had carefully consolidated all his stage coach routes. His company had the best carriages in town, and was making money. He had indeed gone all out with this business. Patrick's freight wagons, and Ian's barges were profitable. Business was good, and he was happy. But he wished Johnny would go all out, and stop drinking so much. It worried Willie. He was afraid to tell Calvin and Malindy just how bad the problem had become. He needed the advice of his friends.

"Why don't you talk to Dr. Morgan?" James said. "Maybe he could give Johnny something for the pain."

"That's what I'm going to do," Willie said. "Don't tell Ma and Pa yet. I need to tell them real gentle like."

Willie knocked on Dr. Morgan's door, and entered.

"Willie, what can I do for you?" Dr. Morgan said.

"Hi, Doc," Willie said. "It's Johnny. He's in a lot of pain, and he's drinking too much. Can you help him?"

"Well, about all I can give him is liniment or whiskey. And I know he don't need any more whiskey."

"The other day," Willie said, "he got so drunk he couldn't hitch up the team. He fell under the two back horses, and one of them kicked him. A couple of the men had to pull him out from under there. I'm scared to death he's going to get hurt real bad."

"Can you get him in here where I can examine him?"

"I doubt it," Willie said. "You know how he is about taking help from anybody. But I'll try."

"Let me think on this, Willie," he said. "I wonder if some of the Indians around here might have something. I'll see if I can find out."

"Thanks, Doc.," Willie said. He resumed his journey home.

On Monday, John started the adoption paperwork for Jenny and Charles. This was a task he enjoyed. He knew this would bring happiness to all of them.

Martha didn't know what to do with Millie. She was a bright student, and learned quickly. But socially, she was a mess. If anyone disagreed with her, she'd knock them down. She was taller than most of the boys her age, and could deck them before they knew what was going on. She'd made friends with three other girls, but even they had to do just as Millie said. Martha had to make her stand in the corner almost every day. But Millie could also gain control of a noisy, unruly class.

Today was not Martha's best day. She had a headache. She was a bit nervous, and dropped everything. Most of the class thought it was funny when she tried to show them a picture in a book, and she dropped the book. But Millie came to the rescue.

"Shut up," Millie yelled. "Teacher's trying to show us something. You all get quiet, and listen. I want to hear what it's about."

The laughter subsided instantly. The class became quiet, and the students sat attentively.

Martha picked up the book, found the picture, and started again.

"Thank you, Millie," she said. "All right class, here are some pictures of New York City. I want you to all look at them. You may stand up, walk to my desk, and look at the pictures. Then we'll talk about these pictures."

The class was polite and orderly as they looked at the pictures.

"Millie," Martha said. "What am I going to do with you? Honey, you have to stop beating up on the other children."

"But what am I supposed to do when they pull my hair and call me names?"

"Which ones have been doing that?" Martha said.

Millie provided the names of four boys, and two girls.

"I'll talk to them, and to their parents," Martha said. "But first, promise me you won't hit them anymore."

"I ain't going to promise no such thing," Millie said. "You're as bad as Pa used to be. He didn't want me to fight back. Then we got attacked by some Indians, and he wouldn't fight back, and it got him and Momma both killed. I ain't going to let that happen no more. Not to me, not to Matthew. Me and Matthew made a deal that we'd always stay together, and protect each other. And we do, too."

Martha didn't know how to answer that. She dropped her head for a moment and prayed. *Lord, help me reach this child.*

"Honey, there's a time of war, when we fight to protect ourselves. And we should do that. But there's also a time of peace, when we try to settle things without a fight. We don't want to fight over the little things like this. Can you understand?"

"Yeah, I guess," Millie said. "But will you help me?"

"Yes, Millie," she said. "I'll try to help you." Martha had a feeling this would be a great challenge.

Johnny raced the horses through town. He was in a hurry to get home, and wouldn't tolerate anything in his way. He turned the corner too sharp, and his carriage overturned. It threw him off the carriage, as it crashed into a tree.

Johnny landed hard on his good arm. He heard the bone snap in his shoulder. The pain was very intense, and he couldn't move. His pants was torn, revealing a deep gash down the bad leg. It was bleeding, and throbbed with pain. His head hurt almost as bad as when the dynamite blew up. He tried to get up, but couldn't.

The horses stood trembling with fright. None of them were hurt, just scared. But the harness was broken, the carriage door was shattered, and the side smashed against the tree.

Big Jim came running.

"Johnny, are you hurt?" he said.

"Yeah," Johnny said, gritting his teeth. "My shoulder and my leg. I don't know what else." Jim touched him, and he screamed in pain. By now, several other men had arrived.

"Go get Dr. Morgan," Jim said.

They finally got Johnny into Dr. Morgan's office. He set the broken bone, and put the arm in a sling. He cleaned the cut on Johnny's leg, and applied a good salve. The doctor checked his patient throughly, and could only find a small bump on the back of his head.

John had an idea. Maybe Little Deer would know of a good pain remedy. So he set out to find his friend.

Two days later, Little Deer brought a generous supply of plants and herbs the local Medicine Man used for pain relief.

"What is this?" Dr. Morgan said.

"I don't know," John said. "He wouldn't tell me. He just said the Medicine Man used this, and told me where we could get more."

"Well, I'll see if it helps Johnny," Dr. Morgan said. "If it does, we'll use this for him all the time."

24 MARTHA'S NEW HOUSE

For the next two weeks, Calvin drove his son's carriage. But he wasn't as fast with deliveries, and didn't know where many of his passengers lived. But somehow, he got through it. Now Johnny was demanding his carriage back.

"But how can you even get in the drivers seat?" Calvin said.

"You just watch me," Johnny said.

He backed up a few feet, and ran toward the carriage. He jumped upon the step, then into the seat. The reins were tied to the brake handle. Johnny bent over, untied the reins with his teeth, and took them in his mouth.

"Giddy-up" he said. Johnny resumed his duties.

"Johnny, how am I going to pay you?" Mrs. Williams said.

"Put the money in my coat pocket," he said. "Go on, I trust you."

She counted out the exact change, and dropped it in his coat pocket. Mrs. Williams shook her head in amazement, and stepped upon her porch.

"Martha, I've been thinking," John said. "I've got a nice sum of money saved up. Why don't we get started on that new house I promised you? Would you like that?"

"Oh, John," Martha said. "I thought you'd forgotten about that. There's been so many things going on this year, I didn't know if we could do it."

"It's time to honor those promises. But this won't be a cabin. This will be a nice big frame house, like they have in Boston. Let's start planning tonight."

They sat up very late, drawing scale models of their dream house, and planning furniture styles. John wanted some art works, but Martha wasn't sure. They discussed fabric styles, color schemes, a room for his law library, and many other things. Martha wanted a new cook stove.

"The hearth is fine, and I'll still use it," she said. "But there's no substitute for a stove."

"I'll see if I can get Henry to help me clear out that spot of land we've always talked about," John said. "That'll really be a beautiful place, when we get finished."

"Can we line the front lawn with flower beds?"

"Of course," John said. "I love pretty flowers, too, you know. And we'll keep the name *Possum Hollow.* It has a good country sound. Don't you think?"

Martha laughed, and kissed him good night. She went to sleep with dreams and plans for a happy tomorrow.

John went to see Henry.

"Sure, John," he said. "I'll be glad to help you clear the land, soon as we're finished here."

"Me and Matthew can finish up here," Thomas said. "This is all inside work, now. Me and the boy can do it."

"All right. It's settled, then," Henry said. "John, I'll meet you at your house this afternoon."

They settled on a wage for Henry, and John went to the saw mill. He agreed to provide the timber from his land to the mill. He'd get Patrick to haul the logs to mill, and the lumber to his place.

John settled in to work on the issues of statehood, but it was hard to keep his mind on business. He only got a few things accomplished before noon. Then he rode home to show Henry what he wanted done.

They stepped off the approximate dimensions of the house and yard. John told Henry to save two of the tallest trees in the area of the front yard, and four in the back yard, but cut the rest of them. Limbs from those trees would be used for the rail fence, front porch support posts, and other decorative odds and ends. Henry knew where they could get the big flat rocks for the two chimneys and hearths.

"John, you'll have to show me how to build a frame house," Henry said. "All I've ever built is a cabin."

"I don't know how to do that, either," John said. "Reckon I'll have to get somebody to help us. And I think I know just the fellow for the job. He helped Dr. McLoughlin build his big house."

"Good," Henry said. "You go get him, soon as you can. I'll get to work on this timber."

John went back to work, but his thoughts were of his dream house. He didn't even hear Mr. Peterson arguing with Mr. Dudley until they were inside his office.

"Hello, John," Mr. Peterson said. "Looks like you're not too busy. I brought you some more paperwork."

"Hello, Mr. Peterson," John said.

"And would you like me to bring you a pie?" Mr. Dudley said. "She's started making gooseberry pies, now. And they are simply delicious. They're right straight from the hearth, good and warm."

"No, thank you, Mr. Dudley," John said.

"John, let's ride down to the new settlement tomorrow. We need more information from them. Then we'll swing up to Salem," Mr. Peterson said.

"Sounds fine with me," John said.

Martha was still having problems with Millie. She had to stand in the corner for an hour this morning, and again this afternoon. Between times, she did all her spelling, reading and numbers. She even got them all correct. After school, Martha called her aside.

"Millie, can you stay out of trouble, at least for a while?"

"Well, I'm trying to, Mrs. Campbell," Millie said. "Just what am I supposed to do when they pick on me?"

"I see your point, Millie," she said. "And I'm going to talk to them again. Is it the same ones from last week?"

"Yes'um."

"I'll take you home, dear. Are you having problems understanding any of your lessons?"

241

"No. I understand it right well. I just don't like being picked on," Millie said.

Henry had worked all day, and had several trees cut. He was chopping off the limbs when John and Martha got home.

"Henry, you'd better get back home," John said. "It's going to get cold as blue blazes tonight."

"Yeah, I reckon," Henry said. "I'll pull all them stumps out in the morning. You're going to have a fine house, John. These logs will make mighty good lumber."

John smiled. Henry got his things together, and left for home.

Martha began cooking the evening meal, while John and Johnny did the outside chores. Martha felt very tired tonight. But one is suppose to feel tired after working all day, and she never gave it another thought.

On Friday, Becky and Billy Joe came to Calvin and Malindy's home for a weekend visit. Jenny and Charles brought their new family to the boarding house.

Martha came by the boarding house on Saturday to help the girls with their studies. Carolyn volunteered to keep her name sake. First she had Emily reading to Marie, and helped Emily with simple spelling. She got Millie to do simple math problems. Then while Millie read to the others from *McGuffey's Reader,* Martha helped Jenny with French.

When Becky arrived, she was visibly upset.

"What's wrong, Becky?" Martha said.

Without comment, she handed Martha her last test paper from French class. Martha couldn't believe it, and she was furious. She read it over three times.

"Why did he give you an incomplete grade?" Martha said. "You got everything correct. This is an excellent test paper."

"Mr. Robinson called me aside after class," Becky said. "He said he just couldn't give me a good grade. Martha, I worked hard in this class, and I know I didn't miss any questions. But he said it wasn't even possible for me to get everything right. And he kept asking me if my husband helped me. Then he said he just couldn't pass me, cause I'm a woman, and everybody knows that women can't learn like men do. Then he told me I shouldn't even be in school while I'm in a family way, and to go home where I belong. What am I going to do, Martha?"

Martha exploded. "Oh, that makes me so mad," she said. "Are the offices open on Saturday? I'll straighten this out."

"They're closed till Monday morning," Becky said. "He done this yesterday, when he knew I couldn't do nothing about it till Monday."

"I've never seen other students treated so shamefully in my life," Martha said. "I'm going to speak with the Dean, and some of the other professors, Mr. Meeker and Mr. Peterson, too. This is an outrage."

It had been a long time since Martha had felt so enraged. She was not about to let Mr. Robinson's prejudice ruin Becky's thirst for knowledge. But it took her a long time to calm down enough to help the other kids. Jenny began helping Millie, Emily and Marie. They finished all their lessons, and Martha headed home.

She was still very agitated when she arrived home. She waved to John and Henry, as they pulled stumps out of the ground. John had Johnny out with them, and he was playing with some sticks. She put more wood in the fireplace, and gave Carolyn her bottle. Once she got the baby to sleep, she began the evening meal.

Martha was snapping at everyone all evening. Finally, John demanded an answer.

"What's the matter with you, Martha?" he said. "Even Henry noticed that you're mad as an old wet hen?"

Martha told him.

"I don't blame you for being angry," he said. "What are you going to do?"

"I'm going to be in Salem at eight o'clock Monday morning, and I'm going to tell Mr. Robinson what I think of him," she said. "This is no way to treat a student. I'm going to ask the Dean if he will over rule Mr. Robinson, and give her the grade she earned. I'm not about to let him fail her. I'll call school out for Monday."

"Good for you," John said. "But let's talk about something else tonight. Would you like to have an upstairs in your new home?"

Martha was pleased with that suggestion. "Yes," she said. "That would be nice. We could use that for a guest room, and perhaps your library."

They planned more details of the new house, and Martha's anger subsided.

After church on Sunday, Martha left for Salem with Becky and Billy Joe. Johnny had some passengers bound for Salem, and would bring her home on his return trip.

Martha was standing in line, when the Dean unlocked the doors to the Oregon Institute.

"Are you the Dean?" she said.

"Yes. I'm Dean Winslow," he said. "May I help you?"

Martha introduced herself, and requested a private meeting with Mr. Robinson. "Then I want to speak with you, Mr. Winslow," she said.

"And what is the nature of this meeting?" he said, as they walked into his office.

Martha explained, and showed him Becky's exam.

"Yes," he said. "I see your objection. This young lady has a perfect score. He should have passed her."

Martha came prepared. She got her handbag, and took out the diplomas and letters of recommendation from King's College in New York, Cambridge, in London, and the Sorbonne in Paris. As he read the documents, Mr. Winslow's eye-brows raised, and his mouth fell open.

"My, my, Mrs. Campbell," he said. "I had no idea. You certainly are qualified to raise this criticism. Excuse me, and I'll bring Mr. Robinson in for a face-to-face meeting. I'd like to know why he gave her an incomplete."

The two men entered the office, and sat down. Mr. Winslow introduced Martha to Mr. Robinson.

"Mr. Robinson," the Dean said. "We have a problem here. This exam paper belongs to one of your students, Rebecca Miller McCavendish. Are you aware that this is a perfect test? Why did you give her an incomplete grade?"

Mr. Robinson cleared his throat. "Sir, I feel it's nearly impossible to have a 'perfect' test score," he said.

"Well, what's wrong with her answers?" Mr. Winslow said. "I don't see anything amiss. Would you please point out the mistakes to Mrs. Campbell and myself."

Mr. Winslow handed him the test paper, and he looked at it.

"Mr. Winslow, with all due respect, surely you don't think that a woman could make a perfect score in such advanced French, do you?" Mr. Robinson said.

Martha gasped. His statement made her very angry. She resisted the temptation to scream like a Banshee. But she held her peace.

"Mr. Robinson," Dean Winslow said. "I sincerely hope you're not implying that women are inferior students. If that's the case, you need to examine Mrs. Campbell's credentials. She's far more qualified to teach this class that you are."

"Impossible," he said.

Mr. Winslow handed him Martha's papers. Mr. Robinson stared in disbelief.

"This just can't be," he said. "Someone, some man must have helped you. Or perhaps these are clever forgeries. I'm sorry, but no woman could have done this."

"Mr. Robinson," Martha said curtly. "No one helped me. None of these schools gave me a grade. I took and passed the same exams the male students took. I had two or three professors whose opinions matched your own. And I had to prove to them I was just as intelligent as the men. But I did prove it, even though they made it very difficult for me. If you'd like, I can give you names and addresses of those professors. You may write them, and search my records."

"No, that won't be necessary," Mr. Robinson said. "I'm terribly sorry if I've offended you."

"Offended *me*?" Martha said, raising her voice. "Yes, this grade offends me. Your attitude offends me. Mr. Robinson, I've known Rebecca and her family for several years, now. I know how hard she's worked, how much she wants a good education. *She's* the one offended and hurt."

"Mr. Robinson," Dean Winslow said. "It is my judgement that you must give Rebecca the grade she's earned, and it must be entered into the school's records." He gave the test paper back to Mr. Robinson, along with his pen.

Mr. Robinson marked the paper with a 100% grade, and placed his initials beside it. Dean Winslow counter signed.

"Now, Mr. Robinson," Winslow said. "I'm writing this incident in your files. If any such thing ever occurs again, you will be dismissed from The Oregon Institute. Is that clear?"

"Yes, sir," he said.

"You may give this exam back to Rebecca," Mr. Winslow said.

He took the paper, and left the room.

Martha was relieved. She stood to thank Dean Winslow.

"Thank you, sir," Martha said.

"My pleasure," he said. "Mrs. Campbell, if you're interested in a career, The Oregon Institute would be delighted to have you."

"Thank you," she said. "But right now, I feel I'm needed most at the Oregon City school. But I'll certainly keep that in mind."

Martha would liked to have seen Becky's reaction when Mr. Robinson gave her the corrected grade, but she had a stage to catch. She smiled, and felt good that justice had prevailed.

She sat beside Martha, and kept trying to watch Johnny, as he talked with the other passengers.

"Who is that man?" she said.

"Oh, that's Johnny Miller," Martha said.

"Is he the stage driver?"

"Yes, he is."

"But how can he drive the team?" she said. "He's only got one arm, and looks like it's broke."

"Johnny's a very resourceful young man," Martha said. "I have complete confidence in his abilities. Just relax. You'll see."

When they arrived in Oregon City, Martha watched the young lady talking with Johnny. She smiled, and went to John's office.

25 FOUNDATIONS

Martha thought things had settled down at school. Millie was behaving more like a lady. She had made remarkable progress, even gained the friendships of those who'd tormented her. Martha was positive she could pass Millie to the next grade.

Mr. Peterson and Dr. McLoughlin scheduled a meeting with representatives from all the communities. John and Big Jim came from Oregon City.

"Gentlemen, I'd like you to meet the man who'll be writing most of the laws for our state constitution," Dr. McLoughlin said. "This is John Campbell, from Oregon City. If you have any questions, please speak to him about your concerns."

"Are you a lawyer?"

"Yes, sir," John said. "I have a law degree from Yale University, 1837, top ten percent of my class. I practiced law in Boston for six years, before coming out here. I can provide a number of good references, if you need them."

That satisfied their anxiety about his abilities. Then Mr. Peterson began to organize the priorities of law.

"First, we need to spell out things that are against the law," he said. "Let's start with the simple things, such as stealing, murder, robbery, and the like. Then we'll branch out into civil law."

"We need to agree on which standards we'll base our constitution on," John said. "Does anyone object to the laws of Massachusetts? Since that's my home state, I know it quiet well."

No one objected.

"How about the laws of New York?" John said.

"You know more about this than we do," Mr. White said. "None of us went to law school. And we've got to trust you, so use whatever examples you think is best."

John opened his law book, and read the legal definition of murder. There were no dissenting voices, and everyone seemed to understand. Each man took careful notes. John helped them spell the words correctly.

"Now, these pages of notes will go in your official records," Dr. McLoughlin said. "You'll need to get a sheriff or a constable, and we'll have to write down what kind of power he's got."

Some communities wanted full power given to the sheriff, while others wanted to limit the power.

"Hold it, hold it," Mr. Peterson said. "Each community will decide what they want. So put it down just like you want it. Take it back home, and ask what people think about it. We'll need a state government, too. See what the majority wants."

"I can see this is going to be a great big job," John whispered to Big Jim.

"I have a meeting with the Oregon Emigration Society next month," Dr. McLoughlin said. "I need to know what all of you think, so I can let them know."

"One thing we need is more professional people," John said. "Such as lawyers, doctors, teachers. We need wheelwrights, millwrights, blacksmiths, farmers, bankers, and all kinds of business people."

"Each community needs a newspaper," Mr. Peterson said. "We need good people from all walks of life."

The meeting lasted well past dark. John was anxious to get back home.

Martha was singing as she put supper on the table. He noticed a happy look on her face.

"All right," John said. "What is it?"

"What?" she said, smiling. She was going to make him drag it out of her.

"You know 'what'. Now, tell me what you're so happy about."

"Pretty soon, you'll have another mouth to feed," Martha said. "Maybe we should make one room in the new house for our nursery."

John stood up, and hugged his wife. Johnny giggled, and his face turned red. Carolyn continued eating.

John and Henry had cleared the land, and pulled all the stumps from the one acre of ground. Henry had filled in the large holes left by the tree stumps, then with his mule, drug a big log over the area. This smoothed it out, and got the loose rocks out of the way. Now they were ready to set the foundation.

Patrick came and hauled a load of logs to the saw mill in Oregon City. In a couple of days, he'd bring back the lumber from those logs. Henry and John hauled up a load of big, flat rocks for the foundation. They got two more loads for the chimneys.

"Mr. Hunter will be here tomorrow," John said. "Then we'll really get things going, Henry. Why don't you bring Minnie and the kids?"

"Well, I think I just might do that, John," he said. "She ain't been out too much lately."

"I know Martha would love it," John said.

John and Martha purchased some new furniture. Martha chose Gothic Victorian rosewood chairs and sofa, a new kitchen table and chairs, new cook stove, and new bed. John got a new wing chair for the bedroom. For his new study, he choose French Victorian rosewood desk and chairs. He'd made a deal with a local carpenter to build two large bookshelves. They got new lamps for each room. The store owner agreed to keep them in the back until John was ready.

Patrick hauled more logs and lumber. They stacked the lumber behind the flat rocks, and began laying the foundation. They ran out of rocks on Thursday, and they weren't even half through. Henry and Isaac Hunter brought four more loads of flat rocks. Then on Friday, they resumed the foundation.

They used the huge logs, split in half for the frame. They had just enough split logs to complete the downstairs portion of the house.

"Looks like we'll be cutting timber for a while," John said.

It took several days to get enough logs, but Isaac thought they had enough to finish the upstairs. Patrick hauled them to the mill, and back.

John helped Henry and Isaac all day, then worked on the laws of statehood at night. He was getting very tired, and often fell asleep while writing.

Martha thought it best to end the school term early. The kids had all learned well this year, even Millie, and she was pleased. But her students usually had to help with spring planting, and she was feeling a little tired. So, she dismissed them March first.

John knew he needed help. He was being overwhelmed with paperwork from the statehood committee. Finally, he decided to talk with Dr. McLoughlin.

"Are there any other lawyers who'd like to help me?" John said. "I'd welcome any help."

"I'll see what I can do, John," Dr. McLoughlin said. "There are a couple of men in the Portland area. I'll talk to them tomorrow."

The new house was going up fast, now. The entire frame was complete, and they began to lay the floor joists. Next, Henry would put in the fireplaces and chimneys.

"John, this is Mr. Brown," Mr. Peterson said. "He's from Portland, and he'll be glad to help you with the legal paperwork we've burdened you with."

Mr. Brown was already familiar with John's work on statehood, and they began their efforts with enthusiasm. John and Michael developed a good working relationship, and that pleased Dr. McLoughlin and Mr. Peterson.

Martha kept meeting the young lady in Oregon City several times each week. Her curiosity was getting the best of her.

"John, who is that woman?" Martha said.

"I don't know her name," he said. "But I've been seeing her around town lately. She must live out of this area, cause she rides Johnny's stage."

Martha shook her head, and went on to visit Carolyn.

The smells of spring filled the air. Farmers were planting their crops, and flowers were blooming. The air had that soft, delicate feel on it's warm breeze, making Martha feel wonderful. She felt a great sense of accomplishment, as she reflected on the last school term. She was so proud of Millie, even though she still had many problems to solve. But Martha began to feel a longing for Boston.

"John, it's amazing," she said. "After we came here, I didn't think I'd ever want to see Boston again. But now, I think I'd like to go back for a visit."

"Really?"

"Yes," she said. "I want to see Grandma Catherine and Grandpa Samuel again. And I want to see if Father and Mother have changed. Wouldn't you like to go back for a visit?"

"Well, yes, I suppose we could," he said. "How about next year, after the baby comes?"

Martha smiled, and nodded her approval.

The letter arrived for Martha from the General Store in Portland.

"Oh, John," she said. "They have my new cook stove. Let's go get it."

"Martha, we don't have any place to store it," he said. "Besides, the agreement was they'd hold it for us, until we get the house built. Then we'll go get it."

26 BURNING OF THE SWEET GRASS

John and Little Deer looked forward to this hunting trip. John still had the buckskin pants and shirt he'd bought along the Overland Trail, and proudly wore them today. But he'd gained a few pounds, and the pants were a little tight. He wasn't about to change his attire now.

"We'll be gone about a week," John said. "We need to find more medicine for Johnny, and I'm going to learn how to hunt like a proper Indian."

Martha smiled, as she kissed him good-bye. Little Deer and Morning Dove said their farewell, and he hugged his children. The two hunters mounted their horses, and rode out into the wilderness.

Martha and Morning Dove played with their children, and Martha helped her learn more English. The bond between them grew stronger with each day. They shared favorite foods and breads, blanket weaving and knitting, child care, and marriage perplexities.

"Martha, why does the white man hate my people?"

The question stunned Martha. For a moment, she had no answer.

"I don't know," she finally said. "But I'm ashamed of it. I wish I could change it, but I can't. I know that's not a good answer. I guess I just don't have a good answer."

"But you not do wrong," Morning Dove said. "You and John are our friends. Our village welcomes you, and John helps us. But we don't understand why they take our land, and kill our people."

"Carolyn once told us many years ago that change must come from the heart," Martha said. "I can't change anyone's heart but my own." Martha cried.

"Only Great Spirit change hearts," Morning Dove said.

"Many white women have a special friend we call our best friend," Martha said. "And I'm honored to call you my best friend. Please don't think that all white people are bad."

"I know not all white people bad," she said. "It is very hard for us to understand, but we try."

"Maybe someday, our children and grandchildren will have a better world," Martha said.

Morning Dove smiled. "Yes, my best friend. Maybe someday."

John was amazed at Little Deer's ability to track game. He could find elk and deer in what John thought was just thick brush. But he was patient, and taught John the art of tracking, use of the bow and arrow, campfires, and many other things.

"John, my people have a custom for our friends," Little Deer said. "We purify our friendship by burning sweet grass."

"You have been my closest friend for many years, now," John said. "You're a fine Sioux warrior. I would like that very much."

As they gathered the grass, Little Deer explained the ceremony. John felt a great kinship with this man.

"You are my brother, John, and our friendship is pure."

"You are my brother, Little Deer."

The children were playing together in the front yard, when John and Little Deer came riding in. They brought fresh deer, elk and turkey. The children greeted their fathers, and began playing with turkey feathers. John and Little Deer took the extra meats to Carolyn's Boarding House, while their wives cooked a feast.

John returned to his office feeling rested, and at peace. He knew the road to statehood would be long and tiring. He picked up his law books with renewed vigor.

Big Jim knocked on John's door, and entered.

"Well, how was the hunting trip?"

"Best hunt I've ever had," John said. "It's surprising what I learned from Little Deer. No wonder we had such hard times on that wagon train. Most white men don't know anything about a hunt like that."

"That's what I've been trying to tell people," Jim said. "Got some news the other day you might be interested in."

"Oh?"

"Seems like the good folks at that new settlement didn't much care for Mary Smith and Henry Gordon," Jim said. "They run them out of town. The Sheriff said he heard they headed for California. I say good riddance."

"That is good news," John said. "I know Paul and Molly will be glad to hear it. And that reminds me. I need to write some laws concerning this."

"Speaking of Paul, I hear they have a new baby girl," Jim said.

John smiled. His friends were doing well. They chatted a bit, and Big Jim went on his way.

The stagecoach bounced into town. Johnny helped his passengers out, and handed down the baggage. As Josie stepped down, he took her hand, and smiled. They walked together across the street to John's office, and knocked.

"Come in," John said.

"Hi, John. How are you?" Johnny said. He looked better than John had seen him in a long time. "This is my woman, Josie Scott. Me and her's going to get married in a few days."

"Pleased to meet you, Josie," he said, shaking her hand. "I'm John Campbell, and…"

"I've heard so much about you and your family, that I feel like I already know you," she said.

"You got that stuff from the Medicine Man?" Johnny said.

"I sure do. Let me get it for you. Have a seat."

John retrieved the bag of herbs and bark, and gave it to Johnny.

"Whatever that stuff is, it works wonders," Johnny said. "We got to go, John. I'm taking her to meet Ma and Pa."

John smiled. Now he could tell Martha the identity of this woman, and what her purpose was. Martha was ever the romantic, and she would be happy for them.

The new house was finished, and the last piece of trim was in place. John and Henry began taking the furniture in, and getting things arranged the way Martha wanted it. Patrick brought the new cook stove, and helped them get it in the kitchen.

"Oh, that thing is heavy," John said. "I hope this is where she wants it, cause I'm not going to move it again."

Henry and Patrick laughed, as they finished scooting it in place.

On Saturday, Malindy surprised Martha by bringing all their friends to see the new house, and giving her a house raising party. Carolyn fixed the deserts and coffee, and everyone brought gifts for the new house. Martha gave them the customary grand tour.

"Well, let's start with the parlor," Martha said. She explained the furniture design, the fabric colors, and the curtains, and the works of art. "And there's such a beautiful view from this window." She parted the curtains. "You can see to the edge of the clearing, and watch the deer come right up to the house." She pointed out her sewing basket, and her new desk and chair. "I love this room," she said. "It's so bright and cheerful." The grandfather clock struck three times.

She guided them through the children's rooms. The love of home was evident in her voice. She wondered if her baby would be content by Carolyn's bed, or demand another choice spot. Johnny got his own room, with his bed by the window. He'd decorated the walls with bows and arrows from Little Deer.

"You all know what makes a house a home–it's love," Martha said. "Without love, this would just be an empty house. But I have the love of my family and friends, and that's what makes it home."

They entered the master bedroom. It featured a big four-poster bed, with Grandma Catherine's hand quilted bedspread. "John loves that feather bed," she said.

Her kitchen was modeled after the one's in Boston. "Carolyn helped me plan this," she said. "When we lived in Boston, I seldom entered the kitchen. So I had no idea how to arrange it. This hutch survived the wagon train trip. I had to buy another set of china after we got here," she said, laughing. "At the time, I thought the loss of that china was a total disaster. But it wasn't. I've learned I can survive quite well without all my pretties."

The winding staircase was richly carved and scrolled. "We'll finish it later," Martha said. It led to a hallway along two rooms. The guest room was still vacant, so they just peaked inside the door. Martha described the two paintings in the hall, and the rich rosewood tables and candles.

When they entered John's library, he was still putting books on the shelves. The drawings Arthur Kelly had sketched of Little Deer and his family adorned one wall, and the ones of John, Martha and the children were on the opposite wall. His scroll desk and chair were new, and he'd purchased a special reading lamp for all those late hours. A mantel beside the chimney held the big clock, and his Yale degree. This room had the same beautiful panoramic view outside as the room below it.

"We'll add more things as we go along," Martha said. "I love my new home."

As the ladies left, Carolyn stopped and hugged Martha.

"You've always been very special to me," Martha said, "And I love you dearly."

"You and John have been the family we never had," Carolyn said. "And we love you, too."

"Thank the Good Lord, I look forward to every new day," Martha said.

"Yes, we all can," Carolyn said. "There have been times when I didn't know if we'd make it or not. I'm so glad you and John have always been here for us."

"Well, I don't know what we'd have done if you and James weren't here," Martha said.

Martha sighed, as she watched Carolyn get in the wagon.

That night, Martha and John counted their blessings. Martha's heart was at peace, and her home was filled with love.

About the Author

R uby Hopper grew up in the northwest Arkansas Ozarks. Born in 1950, the youngest of four in a minister's family, she loved life on the family dairy farm. After graduating from high school, she married Alfred Hopper, and they settled in Hollister, Missouri, where they still reside.

In 1983, Ruby answered the call to enter the ministry, and was ordained in 1986. She graduated from Berean University (now Global University) in 1989. Her publishing credits include two poems published by the National Library of Poetry. In 1994, her poem **Progress** appeared in the National Library of Poetry's **Echo's of Yesterday** anthology, and received the Editor's Choice Award for Outstanding Achievement in Poetry. The poem was used at a local Earth Day celebration in 1995. A second poem **The Face of God** appeared in the winter '95 anthology **The Best Poems of 1995.**

Ruby's community service work has been recognized by inclusion in the American Biographical Institute's **Two Thousand Notable American Women, 1995, The World's Who's Who of Women, 1996,** and **Marquis Who's Who** in 1996.

Ruby is currently residing in Hollister, Mo., where she is working on another book in **The Road of Courage** series. In her spare time, Ruby enjoys music, reading a good book, travel, history, baseball, amateur radio, and all church activities. Ruby has become a student of Oregon Trail history, having visited many historic sites from Missouri to Oregon.

CPSIA information can be obtained at www.ICGtesting.com
Printed in the USA
LVOW05s1128041213

363781LV00001B/74/A